THE HAUNTING OF BRIDGE MANOR

THE TRILOGY

MARC LAYTON

I

THE LAKE HAS EYES

1

"Are you sure I'm going to have a great time?" Rachel had asked the day before she was scheduled to leave.

"I checked my cards last night, and the spirits said it's a go." Alice kissed her thick, un-arched eyebrows.

Rachel had an uneasy feeling about leaving her home. Usually, her psychic friend Alice would call it a premonition and advise her not to travel.

But this time was different. The sixteen-year-old psychic was keen for her to travel and experience a fantastic summer away with her family.

Now, in the backseat with her brother on their way to Virginia to spend time at their new summer home, Rachel felt anxious again. So far, everything about Mecklenburg County was a turn-off for Rachel. She heard cars honking, passed unsightly billboards, and witnessed people poking their heads out of their vehicles to rain abuse on other drivers.

The road was wide enough, but Rachel and her family found themselves stuck in a gridlock. Rachel covered her ears with her hands to block out the unrelenting honking.

"It's okay. We'll be out of the traffic soon." Her father, John, turned and patted her on the knee.

Ben yawned and rolled onto Rachel. She couldn't understand why her parents insisted they had to travel away for summer. Her father was keen on bringing the family to Virginia to spend the summer in a new environment. It was all a part of her father's grand scheme to help Rachel adapt back to normal life.

Monday marked six months since Rachel returned from the hospital after being in an induced coma for two and a half years. Her parents were elated to have her home. But Rachel still noticed the way the family looked at her strangely. She lacked the understanding of how long she had left them as she lay unconscious in the intensive care unit. It was hard for her to cope; everything seemed new to her. The attention. The way people talked to her. The stares and whispers around the neighborhood. And her mother, Kate, always in a constant state of tears.

Rachel had begun to experience strange nightmares, and they distorted her everyday living. The aftermath of being in a barbiturate-induced coma had started to surface, and the situation was difficult for her parents to comprehend. Rarely did brain injuries result in a coma-induced state for two and a half years. Living with her for the last few months had become a challenge for the family, including Ben. Ben had been five when Rachel was rushed from school to the hospital after a severe head injury on the playground. Now he was seven, and conversations between them were scarce as she found solace in being alone. She loved him, but she treasured her time alone more.

Rachel rested Ben's head on her lap. She wondered how he found it so easy to sleep despite the egregious journey.

"Welcome to the Hill Side of Mecklenburg County." Her mother enunciated the inscription on the green billboard they had just passed. "We are almost here, babies." Kate was delighted that Rachel would be able to get out of the city, get some quiet, and hopefully recover more.

"I wish we didn't come," Rachel sighed.

"Don't say that, baby. Your mom and I decided long ago that we were going to take you for a country get-away." Her father's voice simmered with excitement.

Rachel turned her face to the car window. Though her summer holiday hadn't started, she had already begun to count the days until it was over.

"Perhaps we should consider coming here to the country to start school. What do you think?" John asked.

"God forbid." Rachel had learned this phrase from her grandfather. She wondered what went on in her parents' minds to have picked a place in Mecklenburg County. Rachel had researched the town before they embarked on their journey. On the county's website, they boasted about being one of the biggest counties in the United States. She scrolled through several other tales about the county's successes, but Rachel didn't concern herself with these details. She still hated the fact that she had to spend the summer there, so remote.

The road grew lonelier as her father accelerated through the thoroughfare. Rachel still had her face pressed to the window, watching the scenery blur past.

"Look at the fields. Aren't they beautiful?" Kate gushed.

"They aren't, mom. They are just brown," Rachel retorted. Her mother swallowed her words and turned her gaze to the road. Rachel's predicament had been difficult for everyone.

John pulled up in front of their new house. Two men stood out front, checkered shirts tucked into their khaki trousers, cowboy hats tilted to one side. Who wears trousers in this heat? Rachel wondered. The men were tall and well-built. It was evident that they'd spent years in the field, hard work making them lean and strong.

John parked, and they all tumbled out of the car, gazing at their summer home. The house was not exactly the grand old manor her father had described. It obviously needed work, especially the roof. Strung up on the arch, hanging on the pillar, were the words Bridge Manor.

"Why is it called Bridge Manor?" her mother asked.

The men looked at each other, and a strange expression crossed their faces. Was it fear? Trepidation? From the change in their demeanor, Rachel could sense that something was wrong, something they were not saying to her parents, who seemed to be oblivious as they inspected the house.

"It was owned by a Confederate Field Marshall back in the 1800s. His name was Michael Bridge. He also named the lake after himself – Bridge Lake." The first man walked forward and dropped his hat to his hip. Rachel noticed that his smile seemed forced.

"There's a lake? Where is it?" Kate asked in excitement. "When were you going to tell me, John?" She hit him playfully on the shoulder.

"It's around the back, ma'am." The first man put his hat back on, his smile still strained. Her mother hurried to peek around the back of the house.

Kate returned, paused, and turned to Rachel and Ben and asked if they wanted to join her to check out the lake while her dad finalized the paperwork with the men. Rachel nodded, a stirring of excitement in her chest.

"Mr. McAllister, the house is going to need some repair..." the second, quieter man said.

"Not just some repairs. There is a lot to be done to the building," his companion spoke up, gesturing to the siding.

They began to talk to her father about what would need to be repaired immediately, over the hot summer months, to ensure the house was weather-tight for the winter.

Rachel walked around the back of the house and peered at the lake. It was larger than she expected, and she felt a feeling move over her, something like anticipation. It gave her a chill. She returned to the front of the house and stared up, admiring the structure. The foundation to the first decking was built of bricks. It looked grander and taller in a face-to-face view than in the picture. The extended roof towered over the lawn in the front yard, and the porch looked shockingly similar to the porch she often saw in her nightmares.

She jumped and shrieked as she felt a touch on her shoulder, mind still on her nightmares. Rachel turned to see the quiet man a little too close for comfort. Up close, his wrinkles were prominent, and his teeth were brown. It was hard to tell if the discoloration of his teeth was a result of country living or a bad habit, like cigarettes. He dropped his hand quickly.

"Sorry." He grinned sheepishly. She returned her gaze to the house. She had to admit that although it had a shabby look, it was architecturally impressive. The elegant three-story building could pass for a palace.

"Why was the house priced so low?" her dad asked the first cowboy.

"First, it is a colonial house, and we've only had one occupant here since the original owner died back in the 1800s. Second, we don't often get interest in this building because it requires more work than most people are willing to put in," the man replied calmly. Rachel joined her father, and the second man moved closer as well.

"Since you're a contractor in the construction business, you probably like a challenge. Well, it's yours now." They tipped their hats and walked away slowly toward a truck parked in the grass at the end of the drive.

Rachel rolled her eyes. "So this is our mess now?"

Her father sighed heavily and walked to the trunk of the car to take out their luggage. "Come help me, please."

"Is it really ours? You think you can fix it up?" She wrinkled her nose. Her father dropped the luggage at the foot of the trunk and walked to Rachel, hugging her.

"I'm doing this for you. Your therapist believes you need a change of environment to help process your thoughts. He also says there's a good chance you'll stop having hallucinations if you're in a new place. So please do it for me, your mother, and your brother. Promise me you'll try to have fun here." He stroked her hair.

She felt sorry for him. She knew her condition had put the family under a lot of stress, and she wasn't willing to continue to make them suffer. It would be hard to have fun in a house that was falling apart in the middle of nowhere, but she would give it everything she had.

"I don't have hallucinations, daddy. I have nightmares," she corrected with a small smile. He grinned back at her. For that brief moment, she was happy she could see him in that state, cheerful. He brushed her hair and lifted her up.

"You are so big now." They both laughed, and John put her down to check on Kate and Ben.

Rachel breathed in heavily and exhaled slowly. At this point, her thoughts had overwhelmed her. She wanted her family to be happy, although the house and the area weren't her cup of tea. She missed being home. Although her schedule shuffled around being homeschooled and visiting the hospital and her therapist, she found it preferable to staying out in the countryside. Most kids appreciated holidays like this, but Rachel wasn't some kid.

Her reverie was interrupted by a shouted, "Welcome!" She turned in the direction of the sound and noticed for the first time that there was a small farmhouse fifty yards away from the manor. It looked tiny from where Rachel stood. Next to the house was a boy, waving both hands and calling out to her. She chuckled and gestured for him to come over.

"Hi," he gasped, panting heavily as he closed the distance between them.

"You didn't run here that quick," she laughed at him. He looked at her and smiled.

"You won't understand." He leaned forward with his hands on his knees.

She looked him over. He had striking blue eyes and a long muscular body. That build seemed to be a feature for everyone in the county.

"I'm Kenneth. I live in that farmhouse over there, which makes you my new neighbor." He stood and stretched out his right hand to shake hers. There was a lingering pause, both parties wrapped in the attention of the other.

"Your name?" Kenneth finally broke the silence.

"Rachel McAllister," she returned the handshake.

"Nice name. Where are you guys moving from?"

"Chicago, we're only here for the summer." She pushed her hair back and smiled at him. The sound of an old engine coming down the road distracted them, shifting their attention to the road. Kenneth suddenly dropped his hand from hers.

"I need to go," he said hurriedly.

"You haven't even met my parents." She frowned.

"My dad won't want to see me over here." Kenneth turned his gaze to the long road where the car was approaching. Trees lined the end of the road, but Kenneth seemed more nervous as the car's sound grew louder. He turned to Rachel and said swiftly, "Just be careful about your new home; everything is not as it seems." He ran back through the grass, heading toward his house just as an old black Volvo emerged from the trees.

Rachel stood staring after Kenneth. She realized he was scared. His hands had been shaky when they both heard the car approaching.

"Rachel, are you okay?" her mother called. Kenneth had seemed distraught, Rachel thought. The black Volvo drove swiftly to the small farmhouse, and she watched as

Kenneth's father walked briskly into the house. Soon, she heard yelling, and her mother pulled her away from the scene to help carry their bags inside.

Slowly they worked their way inside as the night dropped. Rachel checked the time. It was 7:46 pm. Darkness slowly crept into the house, and all she could think about was Kenneth and his parting words. They itched her ears as they echoed continuously in a low, ragged tone, "… everything is not as it seems."

2

Rachel grew restless on the bed, rolling from side to side. The night was peaceful, and a gentle breeze flowed in from her window. The whole county seemed to have gone to bed; there was stillness outside that she wasn't used to. The streetlights were bright, and they lit up the long road leading to the Bridge Manor.

Rachel was stunned to wake and find herself outside in front of the manor, facing the porch. Her heart was beating fast as if it was about to leap from her chest. She turned around, hoping to see something or someone, as the quiet slowly settled around her. She swiftly walked up to the porch and pushed the front door, but it remained shut. She leaned her weight on it to no avail.

"Ben," she yelled. "Dad, Dad, I'm stuck outside!"

Her heart was racing faster. "Dad!" she called out again. This time, tears were in her voice. They began to trickle down her cheeks as she slumped on the porch. She laid there, wondering how she had managed to walk down and lock herself out.

A streetlight began to spark. The noise was so loud, Rachel felt as if her ears were about to burst. She held on to them tightly, screaming for help. Soon it stopped, a sudden rush of relief burst through Rachel's body. She gathered herself and banged on the door vigorously but was only greeted with silence.

"Sssshhh."

A small voice in the air began to hush her. She quickly ran down from the porch, looking left and right to figure out where the sound had emerged from. Bells began to ring, and she felt more scared than alarmed. The breeze slowly grew wild. Kenneth's words came back to her, and she threw a glance at his house. It looked dark inside, but she ran toward it anyway.

"Kenneth," she yelled as she reached the front door. "Kenneth, Kenneth, please open the door!" She banged on it with all of her strength, not caring if she woke up his father too. The wind grew more tumultuous.

"Kenneth!" Rachel's voice grew more desperate as she banged the door. Soon, the sound of mocking laughter from inside the house made her stop.

"Are you scared?" The voice was strange. It didn't sound like Kenneth. It was unusually calm and mocking, feminine, and there was a strange echo attached to every word.

"Kenneth, if that's you, please stop playing games. I accidentally locked myself outside. Please," she begged.

"Okay. It's me, Kenneth, but my dad will be angry. Let's just hope he doesn't find out." She heard him chuckle and walk toward the door. "Don't make a sound. I'll open the door on the count of three."

"Okay." Rachel felt relieved. The racing in her chest gradually slowed its pace. "I'm ready."

"Okay, one, two...."

The door swung open to reveal a lady with a white, crumpled face. The skin was decaying, oozing out a terrible odor. She clamped her palms on Rachel's neck and laughed. Her teeth were black and dark spittle flew out of her open mouth. Her palms were slightly decaying, and there were holes with maggots in them that writhed against Rachel's skin. She drew her face closer to Rachel's, and slowly, her tongue began to elongate. Rachel let out a scream, and everything went white.

She woke up in her bed. Beads of sweat rolled down her body, her blanket wet. She clasped both hands to her face and murmured, "Another nightmare."

She didn't understand why since waking up in the hospital, she kept having these nightmares. The doctor had informed her family they would most likely go away within the first three months, but she was already six months out of the coma.

After returning home from the hospital, it was difficult for Rachel to blend in with her schoolmates. She even found it hard to communicate with her brother. Ben was so young when she fell into a coma; she had fallen off of her bike and had hit her head on the concrete. After that, Ben had gotten used to life without Rachel in the picture.

She rolled her legs off the bed and walked to the bathroom, her head heavy. She looked in the mirror, her nose dripping fluids. She bent her head slowly to the bathroom sink and tried hard to force out the phlegm.

She watched the water swirl down the drain and rinsed her face one more time, begging for sleep. She closed the tap, and there was utter silence except for the song of crickets outside. Half asleep, she walked back down the hallway, images from her dream flashing through her mind. What if she disappeared from the hallway, onto the porch, and the door slammed shut on her? What if Kenneth appeared as a strange woman?

Thoughts were running wild through her mind when a scream from downstairs sent a chill through her body. Her legs shook with trepidation. Were her thoughts manifesting? Was there a ghost downstairs? Was the strange pale decaying woman down below? She cursed her dad for buying this strange house and bringing them here.

"Who's there?" Rachel called quietly as she tiptoed down the hallway. The walls were gloomy, and the house pitch black. Her father had yet to install electricity as repairs were still ongoing. She leaned on the pile of wood stacked in the hallway to fix the roof directly above where she was standing.

"Who's there?" she asked again. Her heart was racing. She placed her weight on the wood to stay still. "Please, stop this. Ben, are you playing games this time?" She didn't know his schedule – could he still be awake at this hour?

She tiptoed further and saw a ray of light at the end of the hallway. It was probably one of the candles her mother had brought. She moved closer, praying that it was someone familiar. A sudden movement brought her to a halt; a faint shadow moved quickly from the end of the hallway down the stairs to the sitting room. Rachel was certain that someone was downstairs. She leaned her back against the wall and moved slower.

The candlelight went out as she reached the top of the staircase, and everything plunged into darkness. An overwhelming sensation took hold of her body. She felt paralyzed as she held onto the staircase rail and peered at the dark room downstairs. Her mind was whirring. Should she return upstairs and forget everything that happened? Was she slowly losing her mind? Was she going to get caught by some creature downstairs?

She shivered as she felt something behind her. She whirled around in terror and found herself face to face with green eyes glowing through the darkness. She fell back and struggled to gasp for air. Then, stumbling, she scrambled backward, trying to make it to her parent's room.

Rachel banged on her parent's door desperately. She was too terrified to look behind her.

"Yes? What's wrong?" John wiped his eyes sleepily as he opened the door. Kate came up behind him.

"There is something, somebody in the house," Rachel began, panting. John threw a glance at Kate.

"Sweetheart, are you sure about...?" John attempted, but Kate interrupted with a slight cough, indicating for him to change his tone.

"It's alright, honey." She brought out a candle and lit it. Rachel held onto her waist, tears trickling down from her eyes. She was shaking and scared to death. John and Kate exchanged glances again.

"Why don't we go see for ourselves?" Her father grabbed the lit candle and reached for her hand. John was average in height, and Rachel was tall for her age. At fifteen, she was already the same height as her father.

"I hope we find something," John said as they inched slowly towards the stairs.

"It was right there," Rachel said and pointed to the top of the staircase. "I saw its eyes, I was standing here, and it looked at me."

Kate and John glanced at each other again, worry etching their faces.

"Don't worry, honey. Everything's going to be alright." Kate murmured, reassuring.

They walked together down the stairs. John had Kate and Rachel stay back by the staircase as he searched the ground floor. He wasn't taking this threat seriously, believing that Rachel had clearly had another episode.

He returned to the staircase, holding a half-burnt candle. "All clear! I didn't see anything." His voice was ragged, and one could sense the exhaustion and despair behind his words.

"See sweetie. Everything's okay." Kate pulled Rachel close.

"You have to work with your mom and me. Alright, honey? We have to get to the bottom of this."

He attempted to hold in his frustration. It wasn't Rachel's fault. After two and half years of being stuck in a coma, he was overjoyed to have her back. He wanted her to get better more than anything. He just wanted his Rachel back.

Rachel stood in the middle of the sitting room, looking down. "I'm telling you the truth, dad."

"Honey, it's enough. Let's all go back to bed. I'll join you in your room, sweetheart," Kate offered, ushering them back upstairs.

John kissed Rachel on the forehead. "I'm sorry I questioned you. I just want you to get better."

3

The sun rose and penetrated the room, waking Rachel earlier than usual. The McAllisters had lived in Mecklenburg County for just four days, but it seemed like forever to Rachel. Unlike his sister, Ben was having a wonderful time. John was attempting to settle into the area and had planned to host their new neighbors in the yard for a barbeque. Surprisingly, everyone had rejected his invitation, making him think the neighbors weren't very welcoming.

It was a lovely day for a meal outdoors. Ben joined John to help him with the grill while Kate and Rachel decorated the table for a late lunch.

"What do we need those neighbors for anyways?" John mused. "We have each other!"

Ben and Rachel took seats opposite each other at the table outside. Rachel adjusted a vase to prevent the lace tablecloth from flying at the touch of the gentle breeze. Kate carried out essentials from the kitchen while John busied himself at the grill.

To live in a house this size in Chicago had a huge advantage, especially for teens like Rachel. Houses like this were destination points for teenage parties and get-togethers. Since coming out of the coma, Rachel hadn't seemed very interested in socializing. So that sort of stuff wasn't on her radar these days. Luckily, in the middle of nowhere, no one wanted to come to their house anyway.

Kate emerged with a tray of iced tea and lemonade. She slowly laid the tray on the edge of the table and beckoned for Rachel to make room. "Did anyone come to the kitchen?" she asked curiously.

"Why?" John asked as he put steaks on the grill.

"Nothing really. I just noticed that the kettle was in the sitting room, and the candle was lit. I can't remember doing or moving either." She doled out iced beverages to everyone. Rachel always enjoyed her mother's fresh lemonade.

The revving of an engine startled everyone, making them turn in the direction of their neighbor's house. There he was, a tall, lanky boy walking to his father's car. Rachel began to wave so he could see her.

"You know him?" John asked. She didn't reply immediately but stood on her chair so Kenneth could get a clearer view of her. A warm smile wrapped around her face when he saw her, and he leaped with elation, waving back at her. His father, already in the car, took no notice.

"Well, someone has a new friend all of a sudden," Kate teased her, her curious eyes on the black Volvo as the boy climbed into the car and it started down the drive.

"Mom, stop staring at them."

"I believe we are all staring, darling," her father said. The boy caught his attention, and so did the kid's father. He wandered away from the grill to have a proper look at the neighbor's property. It was still incomprehensible to

John as to why they refused to join them for a meal. He watched the Volvo disappear down the street. Almost immediately, a power cable van emerged on the road. Suddenly, John remembered they had plans to fix the electricity and he jumped as if he had just woken up and rushed to the grill. "Oh no, no, no." He ran to get the steaks off the grill and onto the plates that Kate had brought out.

The smell of burnt steak welcomed the workers as they made their way to the family. "It's crazy, guys," he joked. "We were all carried away by Rachel's new boyfriend. Now, look what happened."

Everyone chuckled, except Rachel. She frowned, embarrassed at the idea of Kenneth being her boyfriend. But Rachel was excited to see him and ask about the house and her experience since no one else believed her.

John excused himself from lunch to supervise the installation. Rachel was happy to see them pull out lengths of wire and tools and get to work. Nights were going to be full of light now, and she didn't need to be scared anymore, but besides that, it was high time someone figured out what the house was about.

4

Dark clouds enveloped the night as the men got into their van to leave Bridge Manor.

The whole family stood on the front porch and watched them go. Rachel, Ben, and Kate cleared the rest of the food, and John put away the grill. The men had joined them for a meal, spending their break chatting.

Kate slumped on the sofa, and John collapsed next to her, kissing her cheek. She gently rested her head on his shoulder.

"What a day," Kate sighed.

"I'm just glad we have the lights installed. I pray it helps Rachel feel less afraid," John said as he massaged her forehead lightly. "Where is she, by the way?"

He rose and went upstairs to the door of Rachel's room. "Hey, darling," he said as he knocked and opened it. Rachel was setting up her desktop computer, which was one of the reasons why she was excited to have power installed in the house.

"Hey, dad," she said with a smile. She wasn't sure what cable to connect the CPU to the desktop.

"Let me help with that." John gladly joined her. He took the cable from her and twirled the back of the iMac monitor to connect. "All set, what do you say?"

"Thanks, dad." A warm smile lingered on her face. Her father was delighted to see that smile. He wrapped his arms around her and kissed her on the head.

"I love you, you know." He kissed her one last time before retreating and closing the door behind him. Rachel jumped on the bed and stared at the ceiling after he had left. Her mind wandered back to the events of last night. She got off the bed and sat back down at the table where her computer was booting up.

"It's time to learn more about you, Bridge Manor," she said. She pulled up Google and started a search on the house. There were numerous pages, most of which related to Mecklenburg County history. She scrolled down, clicking on every site as she went. Some pages redirected her, while other pages discussed the tourist centers in the town. Unable to find anything specific about the house, she banged her head against the table, defeated.

Just then, her phone vibrated loudly. Slowly she stood and began searching for where she had left it charging. Spotting it, she grabbed it and peered at the screen, everything seemed blurry, and she couldn't place the caller.

"Hello?" she answered softly.

"Hey, Rachel. What happened to your phone? I've been trying to reach you for the last three days." She recognized the voice instantly.

"Alice." She smiled. "Hey! There was no power supply in the house. It was just installed today, so that's why you couldn't reach me. My phone was dead."

"Oh, sounds awful. I wouldn't want to be in that kind of situation. So how's the summer house? Can I come next summer?" Alice sounded way too excited.

"Come on, Alice. Don't jump the gun here. I didn't say it was a nice place. I'm just trying to make the best of my holiday, but something seems a bit off here, and I can't seem to figure out why." Rachel intentionally didn't mention the strange eyes she saw on the staircase. For whatever reason, she knew it would be a weird thing to say, even to Alice. She plopped back down on the bed and splayed her legs out on the sheets to get comfortable.

"What's off about the place?" The excitement in Alice's voice dropped instantly as if she knew something was wrong.

"Nothing really. I don't want to bore you with the details. The only good thing is the Bridge Manor also has a Bridge Lake. I know how much you like swimming," Rachel teased her.

"That's it! I'm definitely coming next summer! I'm going to Google this place to check out the lake." Her words struck Rachel with an idea. Rachel suddenly realized she had failed to research the lake, and there was definitely a story or some history behind it.

"I'll call you later. I'm feeling kind of sleepy. I had a long day." She quickly hung up and hurried back to her computer. "Bridge Lake." She enunciated the words as she typed them into the search bar.

There were some hits this time. Rachel began to navigate her way through them until she stumbled on a site titled "Lady by the Lake." At first, it was enticing, but she wondered if it was the same lake she was searching for.

She clicked, and an entire article from an online news archive dated 1972 loaded in front of her. It sparked Rachel's interest at once.

There is a whimsical elegance to places that have experienced lifetimes of occupants as if they hide a secret that only the ghosts can relay. Behind their opulent facades hides a skeleton or two. Bridge Lake is a perfect example of this kind of destination. Many locals believe that the house, originally owned by Mr. and Mrs. Michael Bridge, is haunted.

As the story goes, the Bridges suffered a tragic ending. Mrs. Bridge killed her husband and children by stabbing them in the heart and dragging them into the lake. It is said that a dark powerful energy possessed the house. Locals have reported sighting a woman gliding on the lake, dressed in white. Sometimes the surface of the lake appears to stir and undulate for no apparent reason.

Neighbors attempted to subdue and detain Mrs. Bridge but failed. She is said to have eventually succumbed to the same fate as her family, killing herself in the lake, blanketing the water with her blood. A witness, who did not wish to be named, reported that the surface of the lake was covered in blood for eight weeks.

If you visit the area, locals will supply you with stories of the strange occurrences that have taken place in the vicinity of the lake. The haunting of Bridge Lake and Bridge Manor are a frightening glimpse into beautiful but spooky places.

From the pair of "suicide twins" who took their lives in the same room decades apart to the headless apparition of a famous Swedish royal, the dark histories behind these places can keep you up at night.

The article spooked Rachel. She buried her head on the desk, and her heart began to pound. Then she stood, pacing the room, and her mind raced. What was she going to do? How accurate was the information in this article?

She rushed back to the monitor and scrolled down to see if there was anything she missed. Attached to the article was a portrait of the Bridge family. She felt a chill go through her as her eyes fixed on Mrs. Bridge. Were these the eyes she had seen on the staircase?

She breathed slowly and sat on the bed, her mind reviewing everything that she had just read. Her nose began to drip again, so she hurried to the bathroom and grabbed some tissue. As she peered into the mirror, she noticed the light was flickering.

Rushing back into her bedroom, the lights went out. She swiftly opened the door to her room to allow the light from the hallway inside. She wasn't going to run to her parents this time. Maybe something was faulty with the new electrical wiring?

She lay down on her bed and stayed very still, grateful that the lights in the hallway were not flickering. Her window was open, and a cool breeze drifted in. The fear of the unknown kept her awake, and her eye caught a light outside her window.

It had to be Kenneth sneaking over to see her. She rushed to the window and was about to call out Kenneth's name when she saw a figure dressed in a bright white gown that seemed to glow. Rachel ducked down and watched the woman. She held a knife tightly in one hand, walking toward the lake. A tree blocked her view of the lake, so she ran out into the hallway to get a better look.

The lady had a striking resemblance to the woman she had seen in her dream. She was standing near the lake now, pausing, wind swirling around her. Leaves dropped from the nearby trees and began to dance around her as she walked on the surface of the water. The glow emanating from her began to shine brighter.

Rachel used her palm to shield her eyes from the bright light. The woman's arms came up, gripping the knife over her own chest. Rachel's eyes widened, and she swallowed again. What was going on?

The whirlwind stopped, the leaves dropped on the water, and the lady brought the knife down quickly. Movement ceased on the lake. There was only stillness, the type of quiet that was eerie and indicated danger. The lady still gripped the knife, and black blood began to drip from her hands and into the water. At first, it started as sprinkles of blood, and then slowly began to spread through her bright white dress.

Out in front of the house, the streetlights began to spark and flicker. The first two exploded with a loud bang, and they both went off, plunging the street into darkness.

The woman turned her gaze to the house, and Rachel gasped, feeling like the lady was looking straight at her. Her eyes were bright and frightening. Rachel stepped backward.

"I pray I'm hallucinating. Dreaming," she said loudly and then slapped herself in the face. When nothing happened, she walked again to the window, brazen, determined not to be afraid. The lady was gone, and the water appeared absent of blood. She sighed in relief and leaned forward against the glass, resting her head. Her heart slowed, and she caught hold of herself and began to return to her room when she heard it. The scream downstairs, precisely like the other night.

At first, her thoughts flew to Ben, and she was alarmed at the idea of the strange lake lady taking her brother. She hurried down the hallway, and the screams grew louder as she approached the staircase. A shadow moved downstairs, and she paused, her legs shaking. She held the rail with a tight grip, praying under her breath, hoping she wasn't walking into harm's way.

As she reached the bottom of the stairs, she saw the shadow dance around the sitting room. It paused near the kitchen, and Rachel froze and held her breath. The house was truly haunted. She was sure of it.

The shadow moved around the kitchen door and moved swiftly to the door adjacent to it, one that Rachel hadn't noticed before. The shadow passed through the wall and vanished. She ran to the door and attempted to open it, pushing hard, but her attempts were futile. It was locked.

"I'm doing this one more time." She took a deep breath and charged at the door.

"What are you doing?" She recognized the voice of her mother immediately. "What are you doing, honey?" Kate asked again.

"Mom, this house is haunted," she replied sharply. "I read on the internet about this lady who stirred the lake, and I saw her. Then there was a scream downstairs, and I rushed here…"

"Stop it," Kate cried. "Stop it; you keep scaring me all the time. Your father shouldn't hear about this. Please go back to bed, and let's forget about this." Tears dripped from her eyes. Rachel walked to the staircase, paused, and turned to her mother.

"You barely even listened to me." She climbed the stairs angrily, raining curses on the house as she stormed off.

5

It was a bright morning, and Rachel smelled bacon as she walked down the stairs. The rest of her family sat in the kitchen, and she joined them at the table. Kate glanced at her, warning her not to say anything about the previous night.

"Well, guys, there's not a lot for us to do today! I thought maybe we could get some kayaks and go out on the lake?" Her dad suggested. "Oh and Rachel, you haven't introduced us to your new boyfriend. Maybe he wants to come along?"

"Oh my God! He's not my boyfriend. Besides, I need the key to that door." Rachel pointed at the room next to the kitchen.

"That's strange," John mumbled. He hadn't noticed the door before, either.

Her mother searched through the cabinets. "I placed some bread on the kitchen counter. I can't seem to find it."

Nobody seemed concerned. John walked over to the door to examine it. "This isn't on the blueprint. It must be a basement or something."

"Well, I found it yesterday, or should I say today," Rachel said.

"Then I guess you have a task on your hand. You'll have to find the key to the door today. Alright?" He patted her gently on the hair. She nodded in response.

"So where are we on the bread? Do we have a ghost?" Kate joked. "No sandwiches today, folks!"

The gentle breeze returned, and Rachel felt it caressing the skin on the back of her neck. She looked back and saw nothing but the door and remembered why she felt so on edge. This wasn't like her. She wasn't usually afraid of doors or dark rooms until she met Mrs. Bridge, the Lady of the Lake. She couldn't help wondering why Mrs. Bridge had killed her entire family. The internet had failed to explain that part of the story.

She hated the house, but she didn't want to show it. Instead, she remembered the words Kenneth said to her the day they moved in. They still rang in her ears: "Be careful; everything is not as it seems."

"So?" Her dad tapped her on the back, waking her from her reverie.

"I've already tried all the keys, dad," she said. "And guess which one opened the door?"

Her father took the bunch of keys from her hand and checked them carefully.

"You only have one chance." Rachel said.

"This one." John held on to the longest key in the bunch, and slowly he fixed it in the hole and turned the knob. He shook his head in disappointment and smiled at her. "I failed. Which one is it?"

"None of them fit, dad. There is something strange about this place." Rachel snapped and headed for the porch.

John and Kate shared a look. Rachel had been acting strangely, and catching her fixated on this door didn't quell their fears.

Rachel wasn't ready to go back inside of that house and face the horrors within. It felt like just a matter of time before the Lady of the Lake made her grand entrance now that she knew the house had occupants. Rachel looked over at Kenneth's house and saw no sign of the black Volvo. His dad must not be home today. She threw back one last glance at her own house and walked over to the neighbors.

"Press the button next time." Kenneth pointed to a doorbell to the right of the front door. She walked into the house unnerved, knowing his father wasn't at home.

"Would you like something to eat? Cereal?" he offered as he grabbed a bowl from the shelf. He walked briskly to the refrigerator and grabbed the milk carton.

"No, I don't like cereal." She watched him shrug and pour cereal and milk into the bowl.

"You sure?" He took his first bite slowly in a bid to tempt her to eat.

"I saw the Lady of the Lake," she exclaimed, expecting Kenneth to be surprised, but he didn't react. He just continued eating. "Aren't you going to say something?"

He looked at her and smiled. "It's not the first time she's been sighted. Growing up in the neighborhood, I witnessed her stirring up the lake multiple times. So has everyone in the county, probably. This isn't groundbreaking news for us locals." He drank the remaining milk from the bowl and walked to the sink to rinse it.

Rachel followed him. The kitchen was small, and the house was not as nice as she had expected from the exterior. There was no dishwasher, and the floors and counters were linoleum.

Kenneth's house also had a great view of the lake. She could see how Kenneth must have witnessed this woman throughout his life.

"Can you tell me what you know about the woman and the history of Bridge Manor?" She asked, breathless.

Suddenly, the front door banged open hard, and Kenneth rushed to the door and tried to distract his father.

"Where's the car?" Kenneth asked quickly, realizing that the driveway was empty.

"It stopped on the way here; her engine is tired. Old Max says he's going to help me fix it, so we towed it to his garage." He took off his hat and mopped the sweat off his face with an old handkerchief.

Rachel swallowed and approached. "Good morning sir, I'm Rachel McAllister. Your new neighbor next door."

Kenneth's father turned to her, and Kenneth commented quickly, "She knows the house is haunted, and she wants to know more." He looked down, afraid of his father's reaction.

Without a word, Kenneth's father walked past them into the kitchen, dropped his bag, and began shuffling things around in the adjacent room. This was the first time Rachel had seen him up close; he had deep wrinkles and was stout and tall with broad shoulders. He looked like a heavyweight wrestler in farmer's clothes.

Kenneth and Rachel both stood and waited, unsure of what to do.

"I'm sorry. I shouldn't have come here." She grabbed his hand and looked into his eyes. He was the only semblance of a friend that she had in this town. He was walking her to the door when his father reemerged, holding an old shoebox.

"Why are you leaving? I have something to show you – what's your name again?"

"Rachel." She smiled uncertainly.

Kenneth was surprised. This was the first time he had witnessed his father welcome a total stranger. He often scolded him about getting close to Bridge Manor or discussing it with others. Besides, the old man despised conversing with new people. He leaned against the wall, curious to see what his father had in the box yet feeling uncomfortable with the unpredictable situation.

"Dad, I don't know if she wants to see that," he attempted.

"I would actually, Mr.—?" She glanced at Kenneth.

"Patterson." He ushered them into the small dining room. Rachel peered around the room and studied the nooks and crannies. She did not want to be caught unaware. Everything about this strange town was questionable.

Mr. Patterson cleared some space on the table and set the box down.

"Here it is." He sifted through the papers, tossing some aside, organizing them on the table in front of him. "It's all right here."

Rachel threw a glance at Kenneth. He peered, confused, back at her.

"What do you think he's doing?" She whispered.

"I don't know." He shrugged.

"Okay." The old man seemed agitated and excited, and the two kids hurried over, peering at the papers.

They were old newspaper clippings from throughout the years, all relating to Bridge Manor and Bridge Lake.

Rachel seized some clippings and began to look them over. "These are quite old, sir. How did you get these?"

Mr. Patterson sank into a chair, cleared his throat, and leaned back. "These clippings were passed down to me by my father and my grandfather. This story was in the news on and off for decades. Everyone was fascinated by the history of Bridge Manor. And everyone is still terrified, and no one goes anywhere near that place."

He turned his gaze to Rachel as he said those words. Rachel was unmoved; she was already aware of the story. The Lady of the Lake, the terror of the night. She wanted to hear something new. She wanted an explanation.

"The Lady of the Lake won't take any chances, dear. Your family needs to leave that house. Your father was warned but heeded no words of caution." The old man's voice was low and soft, almost as if he was begging.

"Why did she do it? Why did she kill her family?" Rachel asked, desperate to know.

"The Lady of the Lake possessed her; that's what she does."

"I thought Mrs. Bridge was the Lady of the Lake?" Confusion clouded her face as she tried to make sense of his words. "I found an article online."

"Only locals know the true story. Don't overthink it. Just get your family out of that house, or the Lady of the Lake will do it herself." Mr. Patterson cautioned.

6

The rest of the day passed by in a blur for Rachel, the conversation with Kenneth's father fresh in her mind.

She wondered how long it was going to take before the Lady of the Lake attacked. She wondered if her father would ever believe her if she revealed the story to him. She already knew the answer. He would think it was nonsense and conclude that she was having another episode.

Rachel yawned as she walked up the staircase to her room, dragging her feet. Overwhelming tiredness and giddiness swept her entire body. She hadn't slept much recently. She swore that the walls were alive and could kill her if she let her guard down.

"Why did you scatter the toys all over the floor again? I just cleaned them up." Her mother's voice broke through her reverie, jarring her. Rachel missed a step and almost fell.

"What? I didn't do it. I haven't touched any toys. Maybe it was Ben. You know he always leaves his toys all over the place," Rachel said. Her eyes were heavy, and she needed to sleep. Kate frowned and nodded.

Outside, the dark sky moaned and groaned. A storm raged even though the night had been crystal clear earlier in the evening. Rachel was startled awake by what she could swear was lightning. She peered through her window to catch a glimpse of the Lady of the Lake, but she wasn't there.

The strong breeze rattled the trees, and she watched them dance. Voices began to float in from somewhere outside her room, the sound of children playing and running in the hallway. Rachel slowly tiptoed to her bed and crawled in. These were real voices she was hearing. She pulled the blanket up over her body and laid still.

Mr. Patterson's warnings flooded her mind. This wasn't a joke, and she couldn't live like this anymore. The wind blew aggressively and nudged her door open slightly. Her heart leaped in fear, and she covered her face with the blanket, leaving one eye open just in case the Lady of the Lake decided to walk in. At least she could plan an escape from the room.

The lights outside the room began to flicker, and her door opened wider. The creaking and rattling from the hallway made her body shudder with fear. The bulb flickered harder, casting a shadow against the wall. Rachel could see long claws and sharp teeth.

Suddenly the rattling sound stopped, and the sound of children screaming emerged from the direction of the staircase. The beast edged closer to Rachel's door, and the light stopped flickering and extinguished completely. The beast peered into her room, eyes green and bright like the Lady of the Lake. It walked away from the door and moved swiftly to the direction of the stairs toward the screaming and crying children.

A soothing feeling of relief calmed Rachel's nerves. She hopped out of bed and followed the beast. She needed to know what was causing the screaming, and she didn't understand why no one could seem to hear it but her. She was positive she hadn't fallen asleep. This couldn't be another nightmare. She walked by her parents' room and could hear snores emanating from within. Was she cursed? She wondered. She couldn't understand how in three years, so many tragic situations had befallen her.

The beast ran down the stairs, and Rachel followed it carefully. The beast walked through the sitting room and headed for the basement. Rachel stood behind and watched as it inserted a claw through the keyhole and opened the door.

The room beyond the door was dark. Rachel couldn't see anything from where she stood and decided to trail the beast. She tiptoed through the doorway, and the door slammed behind her. She ran to the door and tried to open it, but the knob was locked. She kicked it repeatedly, but it was a futile attempt. It was obvious she couldn't fight her way out.

The rattling sound resumed, combined with loud sobbing. The sound moved closer, and Rachel felt like her eardrums were about to burst. Her heart pounded faster, and she shrieked in pain. She covered both ears with her palms as the sounds pounded through her head. Gradually, she dropped to the floor, dizzy, and a smoky shadow overwhelmed her. Fear coursed through her veins, and she fought back slowly, but she was weak. The shadow stretched to strike the final blow, and then she woke up, screaming and sweating profusely.

There was a sudden sound of quick footsteps in the hallway, and she turned toward the bedroom door. She felt relieved to see it shut. She was curious about the basement door. Was it really just a dream? Rachel checked her body for wounds or scratches, but there were none. Her door swung open suddenly, her father bursting through. He ran his hand through his hair, alarmed.

"You're sweating. Another nightmare?"

She ignored him and hopped out of bed. She could hear the sobbing sounds again. She quickly walked past her parents and reached the stairs. Her parents trailed behind, confused.

Upon reaching the basement door, Rachel tried hard to open it. She slammed into it with her shoulder, causing her father to hold her back.

"Let go of me. I have to get into this door." Beads of sweat dripped down her face.

"Rachel, you have to stop this," he begged her. She tried hard to wriggle out of his grasp. "Listen to me. I understand that you're having nightmares. I know you are still feeling the repercussions of your concussion, but you have to fight it off. Consider your little brother, he wants to have a nice time here. You're scaring all of us. You need to stop all these theatrics and behave yourself."

"Or else?" Rachel cried, frustrated.

"I will send you back to Chicago for rehabilitation." His eyes were red, his face flustered. He stormed off to the stairs and found Ben at the top in his Mickey Mouse pajamas. John scooped him up and carried him back to his room.

Rachel dropped to the floor and began sobbing. Why would no one believe her?

7

Kate walked into the kitchen early the next morning and stumbled in shock. Her mouth dropped open as she surveyed the scene. Water dripped from the countertops, the cabinets were haphazardly open, and shards of ceramic littered the floor. She bent down and picked up a bent spoon. Kate was alarmed. She could recall that she had cleaned the kitchen and the sitting room late the night before. As she had sat in the kitchen drinking a glass of wine before bed, it had not looked anything like this.

Her night had not been easy. She grossly underestimated the extent to which Rachel's nightmares could affect her. After the incident in the middle of the night, Kate recalled the strange events she experienced in the house. The toys, for example, earlier - she had made her mind up to blame Rachel for wreaking such havoc. But time and time again, she could clearly see Rachel wasn't the problem. She realized Rachel had been distant from the entire family, including Ben. But she wasn't destroying the house.

Kate did not subscribe to Rachel's story of strange people sneaking around the house. She and John had not entertained the idea. Her heart felt heavy for her daughter. She knew Rachel was struggling, but things were getting a bit out of hand. Last night's experience made her consider that perhaps something strange had occurred in the house. She couldn't place it - especially as she stood in front of the kitchen door staring at the mess.

"John! John!" She called out his name softly. She jumped over the broken shards of ceramic plates strewn all over the floor of the kitchen.

"John." She called out again, this time louder.

"Yes, honey." He appeared swiftly. "What the hell! What happened here?"

He rushed over to help his wife and accidentally stepped on one of the broken pieces, which tore into his foot. He shouted and hopped on one leg until Kate helped him to the floor.

"Sorry, love." She grabbed his leg to size up the damage of the wound. "It's deep. I think we should go to the hospital," she said firmly. He nodded while trying to keep the pain at bay.

"We have to talk, though, about Rachel and this place," she said as she rinsed the wound on his foot. "But that's for when we return."

"I'm not looking forward to it, but I agree." They exchanged a serious look. Then Kate lifted him, held him by the arm, and led him to the car.

Ben reached the bottom of the stairs, still in his pajamas, and rounded in the direction of the kitchen, his hungry stomach guiding the way. He stopped suddenly. A distant sound grew louder. He quickly traced it down to the basement. Just as the door came into view, the handle started to shake and turn.

Rachel came downstairs shortly after her brother. She noticed Ben standing there, talking to himself.

"You all right, Ben?"

Ben turned to her and nodded.

"You were talking to someone. Who were you talking to?"

"Yvonne, she just went in there." He pointed at the basement door. "I'm hungry," he said, remembering why he had been heading to the kitchen before turning away to stand at the door.

"Who is Yvonne, Ben?"

He walked away and headed for the kitchen. Rachel grabbed his hand.

"Answer me, Ben. Who is Yvonne?" she asked insistently.

Ben just stood silently.

"Ben, I am talking to you, don't ignore me." She was fuming now. She knew this had to be related to the Lady of the Lake.

"She doesn't want people to know her," he said slowly. "She often plays with me."

"Okay." She nodded. She couldn't make sense of what he was saying, but she had a feeling it was related to the mysterious happenings in this house.

"What the—." She stopped short, staring at the kitchen. "Ben, did you do this?"

He shook his head.

"Okay, hold on, don't step anywhere." She grabbed a broom and swept the debris away as best as she could.

"Okay, I'll spread the Nutella on the bread for you." She grabbed a loaf from the cupboard and led Ben to the dining room. She looked at the basement. The door was slightly open. This was her chance to see for herself what was inside.

After eating, Ben played by himself in the sitting room. Rachel found it odd that her parents were out so early in the morning, especially because they left no note.

Rachel realized it was the perfect opportunity to sneak into the basement to find out what was in there. She was eager to go in, but she had to go in prepared. She found a flashlight and then hurried to find her father and Ben's baseball gear because she anticipated some sort of confrontation. Grabbing a bat and jamming a baseball helmet onto her head, she tried to pump herself up. She had to know what was down there. It was pulling her into the basement.

She stood in front of a mirror, padded from head to toe.

"I'm ready," she said to herself, swinging the bat left and right. Then, she walked boldly to the door of the basement, reminding herself that she could do anything. She gave herself a few more practice swings and took a deep breath.

"You're so dead. You're mincemeat in my hands. You hear that?" She latched on to the knob and turned it. She opened the door wide, so Ben could hear her if she screamed for help.

Slowly she walked into the darkness, holding the bat in front of her, anticipating a sound or a movement. The daylight from the open door provided enough illumination at the entrance, but soon she had to switch on the flashlight. The darkness in the room still felt overwhelming in the flashlight's dim glow. As she made her way in deeper, a stench reached her nostrils. She coughed.

"This is the first and last summer I'm going to be in this house," she said aloud. "I will make it out alive." She aimed the flashlight's beam around the small room, searching for the source of the smell.

There was a large iron rack on one wall of the room lined with what appeared to be books and maps. As she peered closer, Rachel could see how old they were, even laced with spider webs. She began to scan the rows until her flashlight reached one that caught her eye. It was a large book with bold inscription, *Major Michael Bridge's Journal*. A map was stuck in between the pages of the book. She grabbed it and wiped the dust off the cover page.

Rachel sneezed twice and then wiped her nose with her hand.

Shining the flashlight around the room once more, Rachel saw a table holding a folded Confederate flag. She moved the flag to the side and set the book in its place, and she carefully opened its cover.

The ink on the book was faded, making it difficult to decipher the writing inside. Closing it again, she walked back to the basement entrance, relieved that the door was still unlocked and relieved that she had not encountered any dark spirits. A voice stopped her at the entrance. It was her mother, talking to Ben. She pushed her way out of the door and shut it softly behind her.

"Who is Yvonne, sweetheart?" She leaned in to talk to him, stroking his hair as he played with his toys.

"She's a friend." He replied softly.

"Oh, how did she get into the house?" Her voice sounded calm but shaky.

"She lives here." He did not bat an eyelid and kept playing with his toy. Finally, Kate turned and caught sight of Rachel.

"What do you know about this?"

"About what?" she replied unhelpfully, clutching the book and map under her arm.

"First, the kitchen. And the water in the sink was running again today. I used the word again because it has happened several times, and we both know Ben is not tall enough to reach it." She looked somewhat accusingly at Rachel.

"I don't know what to tell you, mom. Everyone believes I'm crazy for suggesting that there is something wrong with this house." She said in a huff and walked out the front door, letting it slam behind her.

The room was quiet. Kenneth sat opposite Rachel as he scanned the book she had discovered in the basement. Rachel just looked on, short of words. She desperately wanted some answers, and time was running out to flee from the impending danger of the Lady of the Lake.

"This is like a relic," Kenneth finally said. "It's old, belongs to Michael Bridge, one of the chief soldiers in the American Civil War. It could be that he knows about the Lady of the Lake, but I'm not sure yet."

"That's all you have to say." Rachel frowned.

"My father should know the details, but I don't." He said reassuringly.

"So all we have to do is wait for him." Rachel sighed, impatient.

"Sounds like he's here already." And they both heard the sound of the car coming up the drive and rushed to the door. Mr. Patterson was putting the car in park as they spilled outside.

The older man frowned, catching sight of them. "Rachel, is that you?" He asked, closing the door to his car.

"Yes, sir." Rachel noticed his Southern accent for the first time.

"Dad, Rachel has something she wants to show you," Kenneth said.

"Well, let's head inside and take a look." He offered. "Coffee?"

"No, thank you." She answered, wrinkling her nose. "Look, sir, I really just need some answers to my questions. I feel I'm losing my mind."

"The best thing is to leave that house." He poured the hot brown liquid into his coffee-stained mug.

"Look at me. I'm fifteen. I can't just pick up a car and leave for Illinois," she retorted. "I need to know Major Bridge's connection to the ghost haunting this place. Please."

Mr. Patterson cleared his throat and took a sip of his coffee. "After the war, Michael Bridge was a sheriff in this county. He was famous back then in the 1800s. He is still famous now. Probably the most famous sheriff this county has ever had." He cleared his throat again.

"He retired from the army after the Civil War ended and returned home. He was appointed Sheriff of Mecklenburg, and back then, the county was pretty rich in agriculture. So he was given enough land to compensate him for his service, but he wanted more land for himself. He brought it up to the Mayor and bribed him because he knew the townspeople would be against it. The Mayor decided to give him the land and the lake. But there was a cemetery there first." The old man pointed his hand in the direction of the house.

"The story goes that Michael Bridge had the corpses dug up and buried in the lake. So the spirits of those poor souls wander the land and the lake trying to make it back to their original burial ground." The old man coughed and spat out the phlegm that was stuck in his throat.

"And what about the Lake Lady? How did she come about?" Rachel handed the book she had discovered over to him.

He took the book and opened it. "The ink here is too faint to read." She offered him the map, and he rolled it open slowly. "This is the land your family lives on." He pointed it out to her on the map. It was circled with dark ink.

"Lake Cemetery." She enunciated the words used to label the land.

"That's right. The sheriff stole the public's land and used it to build the mansion, Bridge Manor. Your house."

8

Kate walked past the bathroom and stopped cold, frozen by the sound of running tap water. How was this happening again? She entered to find hot water gushing out, steam filling the air. She closed it quickly and opened the window to air out the bathroom. Clutching the sides of the sink, staring into the mirror, Kate could see the fear in her eyes. What was going on here?

Her thoughts drifted to Rachel. Were they too hard on her, and she was acting out? Before the traumatic injury that landed her in a coma, their life had been blissful. The accident had been trying on the whole family, and had been especially difficult on her marriage. She and John had to endure a fractured marriage for the two and half years Rachel stayed at the ICU, for better or for worse, they say.

Kate stared at herself in the mirror, surprised to find that tears were streaming down her cheeks. She did not know what to believe anymore. Ben was talking to himself and had an imaginary friend called Yvonne. Rachel kept insisting that there was a strange creature in the house, and after the kitchen incident this morning, Kate could no longer ignore that something was wrong in this house.

Ignoring reality is a fantasy, just like John always tried to do. She splashed water over her face and reached for a towel as something white flashed in the mirror, startling her. She turned around, but the bathroom was empty. Was she seeing things now?

"Did you just walk in the bathroom?" She asked John, who was lying on the bed, absorbed in a golf magazine.

"No," John replied, his eyes still fixed on the magazine.

"Well, I just saw someone in the bathroom. If it wasn't you, who was it?" She seized the magazine and looked at him, panicked. "Who was it?"

John was surprised by the change in her attitude. He tried to get up from the bed, but she pushed him back down. "What is the matter with you, honey?"

"Answer my question, John." She dropped the magazine on the floor, paced around the room, and found herself back in the bathroom. She burst into tears which quickly turned into loud sobs. She looked in the mirror and saw that she was a mess. Her hair was scattered, her face was wet and blotchy, and she had dark circles under her eyes. She laughed maniacally.

"Rachel was right!" She shrieked, sobbing harder. Just then, the Lady of the Lake appeared and clasped her hand over her mouth. Kate screamed and dropped to the floor. John rushed into the room as the light began to flicker. He glanced perplexed at the light and then down at Kate on the floor.

"What is going on with you?" He was baffled at the state she was in, laughing and rolling on the floor. John tried to lift her, but she swatted him away. Throwing up his hands, he stormed out of the bathroom, grabbed his magazine, and headed downstairs. The door slammed as he went outside. Kate picked herself up off the floor, made her way to the staircase, and smiled.

Rachel walked briskly through the grass, filled with renewed clarity from her visit to Kenneth's house. She had made up her mind. She would confront her parents and inform them that they had to leave and go back to Chicago. She would present all of the evidence and sound convincing. She had no choice. It had to work.

She reached the front door and breathed in, calming her nerves. The fear of her parents not taking her seriously worried her. She held the doorknob and turned the handle slowly, and as she entered, she heard her mom and Ben in the kitchen. She deposited the journal and map in the sitting room and joined them. "Hey, mom," she finally said.

Kate did not reply. She stood over Ben, towering over him. "Who is Yvonne?" she demanded.

Rachel threw a surprised glance at her. At first, she had assumed it was a normal conversation they were having. Then, she moved further into the room and noticed her mom clutched a kitchen knife, and Ben looked terrified. He held a pillow tightly, tears dripping from his eyes.

"You little brat, you have to tell me who you keep talking to." She pointed the knife at him. At this point, Rachel knew she had to intervene.

"Mother." She began gently. "What is going on? What is the matter?" The lights flickered overhead as Kate turned the knife on her instead. Her mother's eyes flashed green. Rachel gasped as realization hit her. "Ben." She called out shakily. "Ben, I need you to come here right now." He ran swiftly and hid behind her.

"You are the cause of this." Kate hissed. "You pushed us to our limit. I did not imagine my life full of sorrow and perseverance, but you made that happen. You caused it. Everything is your fault." She lunged at Rachel with the knife but missed.

"Mom, stop," Rachel yelled. "Stop. Dad. Dad!"

Kate plunged the knife at her again. This time, Rachel caught hold of the handle and tried to shake the knife out of her mother's hand. They both struggled, and Rachel felt a searing pain in her arm. She looked down and saw that Kate had torn her flesh with her teeth. Rachel shrieked for help, but her father was nowhere to be found. She summoned all her strength and pushed her mother to the floor, escaping her grasp.

Without thinking, she grabbed Ben and ran to the staircase. Her father suddenly burst in through the front door, and Rachel ran to him. They all stared, still in shock, as Kate rose from the kitchen floor, blood dripping from her mouth. She straightened up and pointed the knife at Rachel.

"Kate, honey, let's talk this out. I don't know what's going on, but we can talk through this." John pleaded. Kate charged forward, still wielding the knife, and Rachel pushed Ben out of the way and attempted to block her. John helped Ben out onto the porch for safety and returned to help Rachel. Kate was advancing quickly and slashed Rachel in the shoulder. Blood poured out profusely from the wound. John charged at her and managed to push her away but slipped on the blood and lost his footing. Rachel watched in horror as he screamed in shock, and her mother towered over him and brought the knife down straight into his heart. He inhaled sharply, and his eyes rolled back.

"I want to watch the life drain from your eyes," Kate said to him. Rachel wailed as John took one last breath and stopped moving.

Suddenly, Rachel slammed a chair across her mother's back. She rushed outside, grabbed Ben's hand, and tried to escape in the direction of Kenneth's house. Her mother followed close behind and latched on to Rachel, pinning her to the ground. The knife had fallen to the side in the struggle. Kate climbed astride Rachel the same way she had her husband.

"Please, mom, no," Rachel pleaded, crying. She tried to wriggle away, but Kate pinned her down to the ground.

"Mom, stop," Ben screamed. "Mom, stop it, please."

Kate turned to Ben and noticed the knife lying in the grass. She rose and lunged simultaneously for him and the knife. Rachel saw her chance and pounded, striking Kate with a hard blow that knocked her out.

"Ben, come on." Ben ran to her. She ran her hand through his hair and over his body, checking if he was hurt. "Are you okay?" She was panting hard. It was hard not to.

He nodded numbly.

"We need to go now," Rachel said hurriedly.

"You're not going anywhere." Kate rose from the grass, her fist firmly gripping the knife. Her eyes were glimmering green, the same green as the eyes of the Lady of the Lake. Rachel's heart raced as she understood that her mother was the new Lady of the Lake, and that her mother as she knew her was long gone.

"Mom, please, if you're still in there, I beg you to stop, please." Rachel was poised to fight, her heart racing. The mere sight of the knife dripping her father's blood on the grass was enough to terrify her. Ben erupted into tears again, crying loudly. Kate launched an attack on her, striking the first blow. Rachel ducked and landed a fist in her stomach, then sprinted with Ben in the direction of the lake.

The sky cracked open, and thunder roared. A ferocious wind whipped the trees, and raindrops pelted them as they ran. Rachel could hardly see in front of her. She attempted to navigate her way to the lake through the trees. Rachel ran blindly, holding onto Ben, her chest heavy, her heart pumping fast. Another roll of thunder roared, and she slipped and fell.

Ben gasped for air as the rain beat down on his face.

"Are you okay, Ben?" Rachel reached out to hold him. He nodded and attempted to hold her hand. Lightning hit the lake. It stirred slowly, the leaves from the nearby trees carried by the whirlwind erupting in the middle of the lake's surface. Kate emerged, with blood-stained lips wielding the knife in front of her. She charged towards the children.

Rachel pushed Ben aside and ran towards the lake with vigor, slipping and sliding as she reached her mother.

Kate seized the opportunity and pounced on her in a rage, barely missing her with her angry stabs. Rachel's strength began to fail her; she laid on the grass, wet, with blood gushing out of her nose, the gash on her shoulder, her eyes swollen.

Kate paused and licked the knife clean of her father's blood. Rachel howled in fury and disgust, and she could hardly believe this was going to be the end. She closed her eyes, waiting for the final blow. Her eyes were still squeezed shut when she felt Kate tumble off of her to the ground. She slowly opened her eyes and saw Kenneth holding out his hand to help her up.

"What happened?" she asked, coughing up blood.

"I hit her over the head with the shovel. There was no other way." He pointed to the shovel lying on the grass. She reached for her mother and sobbed into her chest. Kenneth went to console Ben.

"Mom, are you in there? Are you okay?" She wailed. She watched as Kenneth held her mother's wrist to feel her pulse.

"She's gone. I'm sorry."

Rachel slowly lowered her head on her mother's chest and cried. Deep, painful sobs wracked her entire body. The clouds grumbled as the rain eased. The terrible storm was over, and the Lady of the Lake had won.

Rachel, Kenneth, and Ben stood in front of Bridge Manor. John's body lay on the grass beside them, covered with a sheet. Mr. Patterson stepped out of the main entrance to the manor, an empty can of gasoline in his hand.

"I'm very sorry," Mr. Patterson whispered.

"It is better we do this now so that no one will have to suffer the same fate as our parents." She looked at Ben and hugged him tightly. Kenneth folded a tiny piece of cloth into a rum bottle and lit it with a lighter. He advanced, and with a hefty throw, Bridge Manor was in flames. Rachel still held on to Ben, the realization that he was all she had gripped her as she watched the house burn.

Bridge Manor had stood alone, holding darkness within, for two hundred years. Within its walls, dirty secrets were buried, bricks carried unspeakable horrors, and doors shut on the tragedy of the past. Whatever spirits had been roaming there could walk there no more. But, Rachel could see now, there was no remedy, just pain, and havoc.

As she looked at the Manor one last time, she felt an intense, deadly chill pass through her, as if all the cold in the atmosphere had focused into one spot and entered her body through her spine, overwhelming her. She held onto Ben and smiled as green gleamed in her eyes.

II

THE DARK SHADOW

9

Rachel stood facing the lake, her hair dancing in the wind. The leaves dropped from their branches as the wind ripped through the trees. Her long-sleeve cotton gown swirled up around her, and strands of hair clouded her vision. She pushed them aside and tried to tie her hair into a bun. The wind howled and began to grow more tumultuous.

"I've seen this before," Rachel murmured to herself as she walked toward the lake as if propelled by an invisible force. It was hard to resist, and she was only faintly aware of what was happening. Her body was in motion, and there was nothing to stop her. She looked over her shoulder for a reason to go back, to break the spell.

A resounding crack in the air welcomed in fear, lightning tore through the sky, and Rachel's heart stuttered. The thunder roared as she walked briskly to the lake. Her heart pounded faster, like thunder in her chest. Beads of sweat began to form on her forehead even as the heavy wind blew, and thoughts began to run through her mind. *How did I get here?* She turned back and saw the magnificent structure of the Manor. *What am I doing here?*

Her thoughts were split in confusion, just like her heart was divided in fear.

A dark cloud drifted from the sky, advancing toward the lake quickly. Rachel increased her pace as the roaring of the thunder drew nearer. A terrible sight to behold, her heart was heaving with fear now. The cloud stopped suddenly, and so did Rachel. A bright light emanated from the lake's center, a giant ball growing brighter and brighter. A voice, soft and ragged, began to echo from the light. Rachel held a hand over her mouth, afraid. She strained her ears but couldn't make out the words.

"What are you?" she shouted, the wind swallowing her words.

The distant echoing continued, and Rachel stood frozen, her feet pinned to the grass. She wanted to yell again, but the words seemed caged in her throat.

"Rachel, Rachel." The voice was soft. "Come closer, come closer."

Green flashed from Rachel's eyes, and she couldn't control herself any longer. She had the sensation of being split in two as she could see what was happening but couldn't get a hold of herself no matter how hard she fought. Slowly she edged closer to the lake, and she could see two figures standing on either side of the bright light— one dressed in white, the other dressed in a familiar nightgown. Rachel pushed to get a hold of herself so she could focus on the nightgown-clad figure. Finally, the green light faded from her eyes, and she could make out the words. Two voices. One saying, "Come over here, Rachel."

The other saying, "Run. Run Rachel, run."

Rachel's demeanor changed as she recognized her mother's voice breaking through the night air. The cloud roared once again, and Rachel knew it was time to leave. The other figure, dressed in white, stepped out of the light, and Rachel knew it was the Lady of the Lake. She moved swiftly toward Rachel, advancing quickly, her sharp nails outstretched. Rachel felt a scream rising through her, and it was too late-

She woke soaked in sweat, a scream ringing in her ears. Rachel turned her head sideways and looked around the room in a panic. Her heart was still racing fast when her aunt rushed in, calling her name.

"Aunt Christine, I'm sorry to wake you. Another nightmare." Rachel sat up shakily, hugging her shoulders.

"It's okay, honey." Christine stroked Rachel's hair gently. "It's okay, you don't have to worry anymore. I'm here."

She grabbed Rachel's hand and squeezed tightly. Christine slowly let go and kissed her niece's forehead.

"It's 4 am. Come on, I'll make you a cup of tea and we can talk about your dream." Christine patted her on the back, and Rachel stood and followed her downstairs to the kitchen.

Rachel watched as Christine put a pot of water on the stove and set two teacups on the table next to a vase full of red roses. Petals dotted the table cloth in the center like drops of blood. Christine pushed two chairs back and ushered Rachel to sit.

"Stay here." She brushed Rachel's hair again and smiled. Rachel tried to return the smile and picked at her nails. Christine put tea bags in the mugs and filled them with water.

"Just sip this tea and try to calm down." Christine encouraged.

"Thanks, auntie." Rachel grabbed the mug and held onto it tightly, the warmth more comforting than she had expected. An awkward silence filled the room; Christine sat still and watched her, unsure of how to handle these nightmares.

Eleven months ago, Rachel and her brother Ben returned to Chicago with Christine as their guardian. The news story of the murder at Bridge Manor circulated across America. Rachel was highlighted as heroic once the police swooped in after the damage had been done. For weeks afterward, her and Ben's faces were plastered all over the news.

And this was their new life. Rachel tried her best to lay low and avoid the media and their excessive questioning. She had already said everything she needed to say.

Her parents were gone, and she and Ben had to move on. She was grateful that their Aunt Christine had taken custody of them. Christine was well-off, and Rachel and Ben had always felt comfortable around her. The struggle for sanity didn't deter her, and she handled Rachel's nightmares and anxiety better than her parents had.

Rachel was unsure how Ben was coping after what had happened at the Manor. She knew that he still talked to his friends from the Manor, sometimes also saying he saw their mother and father. He didn't say much, but he confided to Rachel that they came to check on him and play with him. It was hard for Rachel, knowing that she had to keep the secret of the Manor to herself. *What next?* The question kept popping in her head.

Aunt Christine was loving and kind and was willing to go to any lengths for her and Ben. At first, moving in with Aunt Christine seemed a futile effort to help Rachel overcome the trauma. She had horrifying dreams and would wake up every night screaming and shaking. However, Christine was patient and willing to give Rachel the time she needed to adjust.

Moving in with their aunt introduced a bit of normalcy back into their life. Though they both exhibited strange behaviors, Christine was positive they were going to change with time. Ben hadn't uttered a word until five months passed. After moving to Chicago, he played alone with his toys. The only sounds emanating from his room were the snap of legos being assembled. Once he had begun to talk, it was mainly to Rachel at first and grudgingly. It was strange, but Christine was ready to love him no matter what it took.

"Do you want to talk about it now?" Christine gently took Rachel's hand and folded it into hers.

Rachel released the teabag she had been mindlessly dunking into the mug and looked up, swallowing slowly. Plagued with bad dreams, Rachel often cried out at night, causing Christine to rush to her room to make her feel safe. It was hell for Christine, but she knew she had to endure it. So she politely suggested that Rachel continue therapy, and it helped. After two months of therapy sessions, the late-night screams lessened. Rachel now experienced restful nights, free of the nightmares. But tonight was not that night.

"Did you dream about the green-eyed monster again?" Christine asked, her voice cracking with exhaustion and something else. Fear? She understood that her aunt was stressed trying to take care of two kids after the brutal murder of her brother.

"No." She sipped her tea.

A sense of relief ran through Christine. She smiled again and gently unwrapped her hand from Rachel's.

"It was just something...I mean nothing. God, I was sweating." She forced a laugh. Christine also laughed. She felt relieved she could share these moments with her niece, that she could be there for her during these challenging times.

"You know, your father and I used to be very close back when we were younger." She gave a small smile, but Rachel frowned, trying to picture it.

"I can't remember much about Dad before the coma." Her eyes watered with tears, and she wiped at them, and tried to concentrate back on her tea.

"I'm sorry."

"There's nothing to be sorry about. You didn't kill him." Rachel exclaimed, a mixture of emotions getting the better of her.

"I know you don't want to talk about it, but I'm interested to know how you and Ben escaped." Christine leaned back in her seat. Even the police weren't sure exactly what happened at the Manor, all of these months later.

"It was Dad," Rachel said. "Dad didn't let anything happen to us." She paused and looked up at Christine, irritated. "I've told you this before."

"I know, I know. But you've been so vague about the details. You told the police the same thing. We just want to help you," Christine insisted.

"It's simple. He defended us and died in the process. What else do you want to hear? Are you writing a book about this or something?" Rachel snapped. She wanted to put what happened in Mecklenburg county in the past.

An awkward silence filled the room again, and Rachel could hear her heart racing. With a clang, she dropped her empty mug in the sink and headed towards the staircase. Memories of resentment towards her father flashed through her mind as she dashed up to her room. It was a reminder for her, a memory she did not want to keep. But for how long? How long was she going to keep quiet about the Lady of the Lake? How long was Ben going to act as if nothing happened?

Rachel sat at the top of the staircase and put her head in her arms, sobbing. It was hard living this way. She felt Christine approach and sit next to her.

"I'm sorry," Christine said, on the verge of tears herself. She carefully wrapped Rachel in a hug.

"I'm sorry that I insisted. I understand it might be traumatizing for you and Ben, and this lifestyle is new to you. I didn't mean to push you. I'm just trying to understand."

Rachel didn't move, her head still buried in her arms. "We shouldn't talk about Dad's death again. Please, you have to promise me."

"I promise."

Rachel stood and hugged her. Christine sighed in relief. Although she was curious about her brother's death, she also wanted to make his children happy. The latter was more important.

"You should get back to bed now. It's almost five." Christine kissed her forehead and watched her head back to her room.

10

Rachel tried to go back to sleep, but she was transported back to one of her recent nightmares every time she closed her eyes. Rachel walked down the sidewalk with slow and timid steps. A crowd of students congested the school's entrance, noise flooding the space. It was pretty unusual to see that many students clogging the entryway. Rachel stood back and watched as the drama unfolded. The students were knocking themselves down, one after the other. Finally, she saw her dear friend Alice in the middle of the crowd.

"Alice, Alice!" she yelled out. It was strange that Alice was in the middle of this mess. She usually avoided large crowds.

"Alice!" she yelled at the top of her lungs. Alice did not turn; the noise from the crowd became louder and drowned her attempts to salvage Alice from the situation. Rachel found herself shouting uncontrollably, yanking at her friend's backpack when she finally got close enough.

"Alice, stop it. You'll hurt yourself. You have to get out of here!" she yelled repeatedly. The collision grew more aggressive. It was time to save Alice from whatever madness was going on. Rachel advanced towards the throng of students, and in a flash, the sky turned dark. Suddenly, all the students turned their attention to her.

She halted and froze under their scrutiny. All eyes – haunting, green eyes – were on her. The students possessed the eyes of the Lady of the Lake. She tiptoed backward slowly and turned her gaze to Alice. Alice looked back with a stoic expression, making her chubby cheeks more prominent. Her eyes were sparkling green. The students hissed simultaneously, and Rachel stopped in her tracks.

A silence drew over the scene, and a rising tension rose between Rachel and the possessed students. She shuddered, and the students dissolved into a big shadow, circling her. A whirlwind grew in the circle, and Rachel tried hard to stand steady on her feet, but the wind pulled her upward. Slowly the wind lifted her midair, and her arms stretched out wide. She felt powerless. She tried hard to look down. The shadow kept rolling and roaring around her.

Fear gripped Rachel's racing heart. The shadow rolled closer, more violently, and the wind tore through the atmosphere, stretching her. She screamed, terrified, and without warning, the shadow rushed into her mouth. Her body vibrated, and her eyes twitched, and she could feel the air weighing heavily around her. It felt like the shadow was piercing her soul. As the dark shadow enveloped her, she had woken up.

Reliving this dream made her heart race again. She had the feeling that she would not be getting any more sleep this night. She rose, throwing the duvet cover off. She breathed in slowly and tried to recollect herself. Tonight was one of the worst nights she'd had in months.

Rachel surveyed her room, illuminated by the orange glow of street lights piercing through the window. She noticed that her door was slightly open. Strange. Hadn't she closed it when she came back in? Then, she heard the sound of running water coming from down the hallway. She rushed to the door and opened it and gasped—the appearance of a wet, decaying woman with her brown teeth bared stood before her. Water dripped from her body as she tilted her head sideways and focused her gaze on Rachel. The Lady of the Lake.

Rachel stumbled back at the sight of the woman, who charged at her and reached out a clawed hand. Rachel screamed, her body shaking. She grabbed the woman's face and tried to gouge her eyes out. The Lady grabbed her by the throat and shook her hard, and she woke up.

Her eyes flew open. She tried to scream but her mouth felt glued shut, and she couldn't get it open. She realized she couldn't move her body either. Her room was dark, the door creaked open, and she saw a dark image with green eyes peeping through.

"It's just another dream, it's just a dream," Rachel said to herself repeatedly, her heart thudding.

The shadow moved away quickly, and the door slammed shut. Rachel's mouth suddenly released, her hands twitched, and her legs loosened. She could feel herself again. When had she fallen asleep? Was this a dream? She ran to her bathroom and splashed water on her face. She peered curiously in the mirror, checking to see if the strange decaying Lady had left any mark on her. She examined herself closely, but there were no marks on her skin. It was hard for her to believe it was just a dream.

Checking the time, she saw it was just after 6 am. Aunt Christine was still asleep in her room. Rachel laid back down on her bed and stared at the ceiling. Unlike other nightmares where she screamed and Aunt Christine came to her rescue, this was different. The Lady of the Lake made sure of it, her half-paralyzed body stuck to a bed. What other surprises did the Lady of the Lake have in store for her? It was strange to believe that she was still suffering at the hands of the Lady of the Lake now that she was hundreds of miles away from the Manor.

The faint sound of the television caught Rachel's attention. She jumped down from the bed cautiously and tiptoed to the staircase. She looked left and right, checking behind her carefully, hoping not to catch a glimpse of the shadow lurking around. It was a strange morning for Rachel, and the day hadn't even started yet.

She edged downstairs, carefully placing her feet, hoping not to make a sound.

The sounds of cartoon characters on the television were more audible now. Rachel was familiar enough with the shows that she knew exactly what was on.

"Street Racers." She sighed.

The light from the television cast a shadow over a person sitting close to the screen. Suddenly, Rachel held on to the rail of the stairs in fear as the shadow walked to the other end of the sitting room, headed toward the kitchen.

Rachel rushed to the sitting room after the shadow disappeared. She turned to her left and her right again to ensure nothing lurked nearby. She sighed in relief and switched off the television.

"What did you do that for?" Ben asked.

Rachel shrieked in fear and jumped on the sofa. The room was dark now that the television was off. The only light seeped from the hallway to the staircase. Rachel could see the outline of Ben standing in the doorway. He walked towards her. She wasn't sure if it was actually Ben, or an illusion left over from her nightmare.

"Ben?" she asked, voice trembling.

"Are you scared of me?" Ben asked teasingly.

"No." Rachel sighed. She stepped down from the sofa, a hand still over her chest.

"Looks like you were." He grabbed the remote and turned the television back on. He had grown more mature since the murder and spoke more like an adult even though he was only eight.

"You should go back to bed, Ben," she ordered.

"I couldn't sleep."

"Why?" Rachel's curiosity was piqued. "What is it? Do you dream of that night, too?"

"No," he responded sharply. "The Lady of the Lake is only messing with you."

Rachel was shocked by his words. He sounded so confident and didn't even flinch at the thought of the Lady.

"How did you know that?" Rachel asked him shakily. He ignored her and sat in front of the television.

"I'm talking to you, Ben." She attempted to switch off the television again.

"Don't you dare," Ben commanded. Rachel felt like she had been slapped. He had never lashed out at her like that before. She swallowed and watched him.

"Tell me, Ben."

"The twins from the Manor," Ben sighed, without paying attention to her. He clapped as the Tom and Jerry theme song came on.

"You still see the kids from the Manor?" Rachel crouched down and grabbed him by the shoulders. He shoved her hands off to look at the television.

"What kids?" Christine asked with a yawn, entering the sitting room.

"Nevermind," Rachel said quickly. "It's nothing. Ben is just telling stories." She switched off the television and dragged Ben toward the staircase. Christine looked on, confused, as she watched them head up the stairs.

Silhouetted against a magnificent sunrise, Chicago had a grace and beauty that Rachel couldn't find at any other time of the day. She loved Chicago as a city, although she felt little warmth on her way to school. She tended to treat everyone with indifference every morning. Most days, Christine saved her the stress by driving her and Ben to their separate schools.

"I've often felt I'd like to live here, but for school," Rachel commented lightly, looking at the sparkling fountain at Grand Park. "The Buckingham Fountain," she whispered to herself with a smile on her face. Then, she turned to look at her Aunt Christine, who focused on the road. She muttered some words under her breath that Rachel couldn't place. She didn't seem happy; her fists clenched the steering wheel tightly.

"Aunt Christine, what's wrong?" Rachel turned in her direction. Christine glanced at her and forced a smile.

"Nothing, just work."

"Okay." Rachel looked back out at the road.

Christine looked at her fully, a frown on her face. "Actually, it's not okay. It's not. What happened this morning is beyond me. You lied to me. Ben was talking about seeing imaginary people, and you told me not to mind. How do you expect me to react to that?"

Rachel attempted to respond, but Christine wasn't finished. Christine was kind, but when she was overwhelmed, she began to rant. Rachel had already seen this happen a few times. She let her aunt ramble on angrily.

"Every night, you have nightmares. It scares me, but I'm trying to help you through whatever you need to process. I'm trying to be there for you. Am I doing something that prevents you from telling me what's going on?"

"No, Aunt Christine," Rachel said in a defeated voice. "Ben has imaginary friends. It's normal, and there's nothing to worry about. I'm glad you brought this up after we dropped him off. I don't want him feeling weird about himself." Rachel plastered a fake smile on her face as the car pulled up in front of the school. She turned and looked at the entrance, nearly empty, quite different from her dream.

"I'm sorry," she apologized, glancing at her aunt. Rachel hopped out quickly and saw Alice headed inside.

"Rachel," Christine called out. She smiled tiredly. "Have a nice day."

Christine knew children Ben's age shouldn't be talking to themselves all day long. Ben was eight, for Christ's sake, she thought. She was going to let this one slide, but she had an obligation to raise them, and she was going to do it at all costs, which meant sorting out what was going on with her nephew.

Rachel ran swiftly to meet Alice as they both approached the entrance door. "Alice, wait up!" Rachel jogged towards her.

Alice turned and smiled. "Rachel!"

"Hey, there is something I want to tell you before the class starts." Rachel leaned against the wall. Alice had some psychic abilities, and she wanted to get her best friend's opinion.

"What now? I already told you I can't interpret dreams, if you're on about that again. My grandma has said predictions are often made from cards and fingers and palms. But dreams, no, that is a no go." Alice rolled her eyes playfully and turned to move swiftly to class.

"No, that's not it. Ben's been talking about seeing the twins, the same ones from the Manor. I don't think he's lying, and if he's not, this proves my theory," she said sharply as they walked fast toward their first period, not wanting to be late.

"What theory?"

"That I pissed off the Lady of the Lake. I thought everything ended in the Manor, but it hasn't. Last night, I dreamt of her choking me. The other night, a huge shadow circled me and tried to enter me like it wanted to possess me. I can't stop thinking about it."

Alice turned sharply and looked at her. "Possession is a strong word."

"I know, I know. I don't know how else to describe it. I don't know what to think." Rachel sighed.

"Well, first, you can think about passing biology." Alice pointed to the door of the class right in front of them.

"Ugh. I hate biology," Rachel muttered and walked into the classroom, right behind Alice. They both sat close to each other, with Alice in the second row and Rachel right behind her.

"Ben confirmed it. He wasn't obvious about it, but he confirmed it," Rachel whispered to Alice from the back. Alice turned and peered at Rachel.

"Does your aunt know?"

"No. She's definitely suspicious, though. It sounds crazy, and she's already so freaked out by my nightmares," Rachel commented.

"Good. Let's talk about this more after school today."

11

Using the rearview mirror to touch up her lipstick, Christine caught sight of Ben's teacher leading him toward the car.

"Thank you." She grinned as the teacher stopped by the driver's side window.

"Good afternoon, ma'am." He smiled.

"Good afternoon." She waited since he didn't make a move to leave.

"Ma'am, your presence is required in the principal's office. We wanted to call you this morning, but we figured since you pick him up every day from school, we would talk to you when you arrive."

"I hope there's no problem." Her smile transformed into a grimace.

"I'm sorry to say, but there is," he said quietly as Ben fiddled with a strap on his backpack, not meeting her eyes.

She swallowed, pulled the key out of the ignition, and turned to Ben. He looked at the dashboard like nothing happened.

"Alright, come on, Ben," she said with a sigh.

The teacher led the way to the principal's office. A gentle knock on the door and the principal quickly ushered them in.

"Miss McAllister, we were expecting you." He nodded as he sank back into his seat.

"Okay, I'm a little lost right now...this is the first I'm hearing of any issues with Ben," she said in a low tone, almost to the point of tears. Then, she turned and looked at her nephew again as he swung his legs up and down as he sat on the chair.

"Unfortunately, Miss McAllister, your nephew stole some items from his fellow classmates during class today," the principal said, folding his hands in front of him.

"I didn't steal," Ben retorted quietly. Christine's eyes widened; he didn't speak often, and this problem with authority was new.

"Hey Ben, it's going to be okay. We'll get to the bottom of this." She ran her hand through his hair to calm him down. The frown began to wear off and her face took a more serious expression, her chin hard. "He said he didn't steal."

"Yes, he said that repeatedly. But he was found with four boys' lunches stored away in his bag." The principal folded his arms and relaxed back into his chair.

"Can you explain this, Ben?" She turned red in embarrassment.

The teacher answered instead. "He claims it was 'the twins.' There are no twins in his class." Christine stared at him in surprise.

"I'm not claiming; they are my friends. You just can't see them," Ben muttered.

"This is not the first time, actually. He often sits alone and plays with his friends, imaginary friends."

"You seem to have a problem with students playing on their own," Christine retorted, defending Ben.

"Look, I understand that he's under your care now, and he's been through a very traumatic experience. Stealing and lying will not be tolerated at this school, no matter the circumstance. If this behavior continues, we will have to take action. Have you considered finding a therapist? A specialist would probably be a lot of help." The principal handed a pamphlet to Christine, who sat numbly.

They walked to the car, Christine rubbing the top of Ben's head softly. Ben's teacher quickly called out after her, "Miss, please can I talk to you?"

"Ben, stay in the car." She kissed his forehead as he pulled himself up into the seat. "There's something else?" She looked the teacher squarely in the face.

"I'm concerned about him. He is a bright student, but I believe he has..." He paused.

Christine raised her brow and looked at him. "Yes?"

"I believe he might have a personality disorder," he said.

"Oh, God," Christine exclaimed, laughing uncertainly. "Really?"

"I am not joking here. I watch him every day in class. He talks to the air, and other students stay away from him because of his behavior. This may have been something that was dormant but was triggered by the traumatic events of last year. I believe it would be better to address it now before it's too late." He turned quickly and headed back to the school building.

Christine paused. She looked at Ben sitting in the car and a sudden rush of confusion filled her. She knew Rachel wouldn't take it well if she considered taking him to therapy.

She opened the driver's side door and slid in, glancing at her nephew in the rearview mirror.

"Don't believe them. I don't steal. Okay, there are twins I play with, and they took the meals, not me." He drummed his fingers on the car window.

"It's okay, Ben." She was lost in thought.

The clouds grew dark and lightning cracked the sky. Thick, heavy drops of rain hit the windshield, dragging her out of her introspection. She turned toward home.

Dashing across the car park, Christine and Ben made it into the apartment building without becoming thoroughly drenched. Scooter, Christine's dog, welcomed them with joyful barks, licking Christine's ears and face in delight.

Rachel and Alice, who had come over to hang out after school, walked down the staircase to meet them. Ben walked quickly and hugged his sister, then headed to his room without a word.

"What happened? What took you guys long? I'm starving," Rachel complained.

"You're sixteen. Fix yourself some food." Christine glanced up at the clock. It was already half past 5.

"You didn't answer me - what happened?" Rachel reached out to help Christine with her handbag, and the dog barked at her viciously. She threw a glance at the dog and looked back at Christine.

"Scooter has never liked me. Alice, he almost bit me the first day I stepped in the house."

Christine laughed, downplaying the incident. "Stop being so dramatic, Rachel. It was barely a nibble. He just takes some time to warm up to people." She walked over to the counter and grabbed a dog treat, and tossed one to Scooter.

"Ben had a bad day at school," she said, finally. Rachel looked at Alice, signaling her to head to Rachel's room so that she could have a private conversation with her aunt. Alice smiled at Christine. They both hadn't said a word to each other, but Christine liked Alice, and watched the girl head upstairs.

"What happened with Ben?" Rachel stood close to Christine, who gestured to the table, indicating that they should sit down. The dog returned and circled Christine. She knelt and picked him up.

"I'm stuck with a dilemma right now." Christine looked at Rachel, seriousness lining her face.

"What happened?" she asked curiously.

"Ben stole some of his classmates' lunches and blamed it on some friends. Imaginary friends, the same friends you say I shouldn't be bothered about." She sighed in frustration. "Now the principal believes he has a personality disorder, and I should take him to see a specialist." She finally let herself relax enough to cry, tears trickling down her face.

"They can't be serious. You know he doesn't have a mental illness. He is just dealing with the trauma from last year. I don't think he should go to a professional. He's been through enough already."

"And why not?" Christine wiped her eyes. "I'm your guardian, remember."

"Doesn't mean you know what's best for us. Ben is not going to see a shrink, not my brother. So you should consider talking to him instead of trusting everything his teachers say," Rachel spewed angrily.

"Now you're just being rude for no reason," Christine warned.

Rachel took a breath and tried to calm down. "I'm sorry. Sometimes I just get so overwhelmed when it comes to Ben. I'm too protective of him."

"I understand." Christine gently rubbed her back.

"I'll talk to him and see if I can help, but please don't take him to see a shrink. It will only make him feel weird about himself. He's been through enough already."

"I won't if you can talk him out of it." Christine's alarm rang. She looked at her phone. It was almost 6 pm. "I've got to go. I have a meeting." She pulled out paperwork from her bag. "Enjoy your evening with Alice." She walked off to the stairs and headed to her room.

Rachel pushed her chair back into the table, pondering how she could salvage this whole mess. First, she had to talk to Ben, to wake him up to the fact that these friends were not real. There was no other way. It was apparent that the haunting from the Manor house had not ended in Mecklenburg County.

12

A clock chimed and the distant sound of howling permeated the night air. The sky was dark, and Rachel slept uneasily. It was just after midnight and the now-familiar bright ball-shaped light slowly slid into her room as she rolled restlessly on the bed. The light positioned itself at the center of the bed, above the duvet Rachel slept under. There was enough space between them, the glow grew brighter, and its light startled Rachel as she woke from sleep.

The light dipped lower and squared up with Rachel, then moved to the door. She rose from the bed swiftly and followed the light to the hallway. This time she wasn't scared. She wasn't curious. She felt some sort of connection to the light, like it wanted to reveal something to her.

The house was dark, but light shone so brightly that it lit up the entire hallway leading to the stairway. As they passed her aunt's room, Rachel wondered if the light would wake her. She imagined her aunt walking through the hallway with a light leading her. The thought quickly faded as she approached the staircase and the glowing ball moved slowly to the lower level, as if beckoning Rachel to follow. But she stayed back, watching it warily as it progressed. Once the light reached the sitting room it stopped, suspended in midair, it's light pulsing, glowing brightly.

Rachel took her first step. Her eyes were empty, and she walked blindly forward toward the light. Why was this light calling her? Was it the Lady of the Lake? Was it her mother's spirit? She thought of Kenneth, her one friend in Mecklenburg county. Kenneth's father was certain that the Manor and the lake were cursed because they had disturbed the land of the dead. What if her mother's soul haunted her?

As she drew nearer, the light circled the room, slowly at first and then increasing in speed.

"No," Rachel shouted, stretching her hands out to stop it from going any further. The light moved towards the wall where the television was stationed, and Rachel noticed for the first time that a mirror hung there.

"That wasn't there before," she muttered to herself. She walked closer, and the light wavered, hanging suspended above the mirror. She reached out and touched the smooth surface.

"There is nothing special about this mirror. Why did you bring me here?" She looked at the light and stepped back, creating a space between her and the mirror. She peered into the depths of the mirror and stared at her reflection. She smiled. She wasn't sure why she did. Force of habit? She wasn't even sure why she stood there waiting for the light to lead her to do God knows what.

The sound of rain woke her from her reverie. She looked to the window and watched as the drops of rain hit the glass and rolled down. Thunder roared in the distance, and a flash of lightning drew Rachel's attention back to the mirror. Had the flash been outside in the darkness or inside this room? She peered into the mirror with curiosity, and the lightning flashed again. Immediately, her mother's image appeared behind her next to the Lady of the Lake, white garments dripping wet. They began to move towards her in the reflection and fear nearly paralyzed her. She shouted, and light flooded the room.

She blinked, confused, and saw her aunt standing by the light switch.

"Rachel? What are you doing down here?" Christine turned and looked at the clock. It was 2 am. "Did you have another nightmare?" She asked, concerned. Rachel didn't respond. She looked around the sitting room, still in a shock, hoping to find the mirror.

"What are you looking for?" Christine sighed with exhaustion.

"There was a mirror here. I saw it." Rachel shivered, pointing in the direction of the television.

"Sweetie, I think you're confused. There's never been a mirror there. You're worrying me."

Christine was peering at her with sadness and desperation. Rachel didn't want to have any deep discussions tonight and turned to head back upstairs to her room.

Christine knew she should have responded with more compassion, but it was late, and she was tired. She watched Rachel's door shut behind her with a sad expression on her face.

Morning arrived too soon, and Rachel awoke to the sound of a car honking outside. It was Saturday, so there was no rush to get out of bed. It took time before Rachel was fully awake, and she laid there thinking about what she'd seen the night before. Her mother and the Lady of the Lake were in the reflection of the mirror. This time, she was sure it wasn't a dream. She saw them there, with her own eyes.

Why was she still living in this nightmare? Why were she and Ben chosen to live through this? Rachel tried hard to reason what connection had been established between her and the Lady of the Lake. Was it because she survived? Do ghosts continue to hunt people down, even after they've escaped?

Rachel was at a loss. She stared at the ceiling. A gentle knock sounded at her door.

"Ben?" Rachel asked.

"No, it's me, Christine." Her aunt's voice was low. "Mind if I come in?"

"Yeah, you can."

"I've got a letter for you. From a boy, it looks like." She gave Rachel a sly smile, as if she had forgotten the mirror incident from the previous night. Rachel grabbed the letter and turned away from her aunt, her facial expression stoic. Christine smiled sheepishly and stepped out. Rachel looked down to find Kenneth's name written on the letter. She smiled as she tore open the envelope and unfolded the paper to read:

Dear Rachel,

It's been a long time since we've been in touch. I remember we both promised to send each other letters till we meet again. I really hope that will be soon. Sorry for the delay in writing to you. If you need to call you can call me on this line - 915-6745.

I hope to hear from you soon.

Kenneth

Rachel grabbed her phone swiftly and dialed the number.

"Hello?" she said in a soft tone. "Kenneth, it's me, Rachel."

There was a loud exclamation on Kenneth's end and then an exaggerated exchange of greetings. Kenneth's father happened to be there with him, so the phone was on the loudspeaker so they could all talk.

"So, what's going on with you? We saw you on the news for weeks. We know it's got to be tough dealing with everything that happened," Kenneth's father said.

"I'm glad I got your letter." Rachel sighed. "There have been some recent developments."

"Developments?" Kenneth asked, confused. "What's been going on?"

Rachel proceeded to tell them about the dreams she kept having involving her mother and the Lady of the Lake. The recollections poured out of her, and she felt immensely relieved to have someone to talk to who would understand.

Kenneth and his father were dumbfounded. They had never heard or witnessed anything like that about the Lady of the Lake, especially not so far away from the Manor.

"Are you still there?" Rachel asked, her voice shaking.

"Yes, we are, dear," the old man finally said. "I'm just confused. There has never been an experience like this before."

"So, what do you think?" she asked curiously.

"As strange as it may sound, it sounds like your mother is trying to reach out to you. One way or the other. Maybe it would be helpful to revisit the Manor. Of course, you're welcome to come visit us any time and we can figure this out together."

"My aunt won't let me. She believes that place would trigger the trauma and make these nightmares even worse, and she might be right."

"Okay." He paused. "Just promise us you'll be careful."

"Thank you, sir. Kenneth, I have to go now," she said politely.

"Alright. Just call us anytime you need to talk, okay?"

"Okay, bye Mr. Patterson, bye Kenneth."

She dropped the phone and laid back on her bed. She thought of the possibility that her mother was trying to communicate with her. Was she concerned with how badly things were going between her and Ben? There were so many unknowns at this point, but she was certain she needed to get to the bottom of this.

13

MECKLENBURG COUNTY 1868

Major Michael Bridge was not crazy.
He did, on occasion, like to slip into the past, and relive his favorite days. Days that were undoubtedly more exhilarating than those he was living at present. But contrary to the belief of his detractors, he was able to separate fiction from reality. Usually, the problem with this fact was that it was boring for the old Major. Things hadn't been easy after the war for Confederate soldiers, and he didn't want to run away, didn't want to settle. He wanted the land that he deserved, and he was willing to fight for it.

One year ago, Michael had returned to Virginia after his loss against the Union Army. While he was revered by many in his county, the tides were shifting. Despite everything, he still thought of himself as a national hero. He felt like the country owed him a debt and he wanted to be paid in land. Fortunately, he had friends in high places and a few tricks up his sleeve.

The old soldier had a specific plot of land in mind, and he dreamed of living on a big beautiful lake. The problem was that many dead townspeople were buried on this land, and his fight to get the deed in his name was gaining a lot of interest. People thought he was crazy, and people were vehemently against his pursuit. He was slowly collecting enemies, but he didn't care, as long as he got what he wanted, what he deserved.

Fortunately for the Major, unfortunately for the townspeople, the town's mayor was a dear old friend, and he owed Michael a favor. In fact, they were such good friends that Michael had a luncheon scheduled at the mayor's house that very afternoon. He was going to make his case and finalize the paperwork for that land.

As he approached the mayor's manor, he was surprised to see a crowd of people out front. Word of his lunch had evidently gotten around, and the townspeople were determined to have their say in the matter. As he made his way up the drive, new energy spread through the crowd. They started pointing fingers and shouting angrily.

He strode confidently towards them, hands stretched out wide, beckoning for them to calm down. He cleared his throat loudly, and they quieted enough to allow him to speak. He looked into the crowd and took them in. His striking blue eyes highlighted his face, and he was handsome for a man in his fifties.

"Thank you. You all know, I fought hard in the trenches for what was best for this country. I watched men die in war, and I nearly got killed myself. One of the lessons I took from serving was that life is not guaranteed, and therefore we should live life to the fullest. I will not let my American dream die, and I deserve to be compensated for my service to this country, no matter who won. I made great sacrifices, and now this is a sacrifice that this county, this land, owes me in return."

As he finished, the noise from the crowd began to grow again. People called out in disagreement with angry slurs. Michael pushed past the frenzied crowd and entered the mayor's manor.

The luncheon went as planned, and as the dessert dishes were cleared and drinks were poured, Michael called in his favor and the deal was done.

"Well, you have what you wanted. Tomorrow the headlines will spin colorful words about you and your new land ownership by the lake. I hope you know what you're getting yourself into. Consider this debt paid." The mayor shook his head and took a sip of his whiskey.

"Thank you very much, sir. I will build the finest manor this town has ever seen. My wife will be very pleased." Michael nodded smugly.

The mayor locked eyes with Michael and said, "You are choosing willingly to displace the dead. I hope you are not so naive to think that there won't be consequences."

Michael laughed, patted his slicked hair, put on his hat, and walked briskly outside.

14

Strolling around the neighborhood was giving Rachel some much-needed reprieve from being inside the apartment. She knew she should probably return home, but thoughts of Scooter made her do another lap. As she approached the apartment building and buzzed herself in, Scooter was waiting, barking at her. She locked the door swiftly and charged at him, making him scamper back to Christine's room.

She was bothered by the fact that the dog didn't like her. On the other hand, he seemed to enjoy Ben, clinging to him as soon as they had first arrived at Aunt Christine's. Maybe Scooter was drawn to Ben's silence. Whatever it was, they both adored each other.

She walked to the fridge and took out the carton of orange juice, pouring herself a glass. Chilly from her walk, and now chillier from the cold juice, she decided a hot bath was in order. She walked upstairs, stripped, and turned on the tap. The bathtub was large and sat opposite the mirror and the sink. Into the running water, she poured bubble bath to create some foam. She waded into the water gingerly, the foam rising around her. She rested her head at the edge of the tub, closed her eyes, and breathed in.

"Mmmm." For a long time, Rachel had not experienced this much peace. Then, as the water stilled around her, she drifted away and straight to Mecklenburg County in her dream.

She stood in front of a graveyard in a vast land. Behind the cemetery, giant trees lined the clearing, and she could hear primal animal sounds deep within. But, in the cemetery, all was silent.

Rachel walked through the graves, enjoying the peace and serenity she felt. Something about this place was familiar, and she glanced back toward the road she had come from. It was empty. She was the only living soul for miles. She turned back, walked between the graves, and watched as birds took flight from the woods as she drew nearer.

A chill had settled into the air, and thick fog soaked the atmosphere. She could no longer see clearly into the woods. She advanced anyways, hugging her body for warmth. She felt grateful to be wearing long sleeves to shelter her from the cold, even just a little bit.

A swarm of sparrows took to the sky, an angry buzzing black cloud undulating eerily.

A few broke off and darted in her direction. She jumped back in confusion and dashed into the trees, trying to escape. Inside the woods, she peered around and was relieved to find that the trees didn't look as menacing once she was among them. The bird's sounds echoed through the trees, and she took refuge behind a large stump. It was so cold now, and she was shaking uncontrollably.

A cry sounded in the distance, and Rachel stood up alarmed, trying to pinpoint where the noise was coming from. It felt like time and distance no longer mattered. She took a tentative step forward in the direction she thought the sound was coming from and stumbled back in shock. She was suddenly at the edge of the lake. The cries were louder now, and what she saw in the lake made her blood run cold.

Her mother, Kate, floated in the middle of the lake, arms outstretched, crying out for help. She knew she should swim out into the water and help, but she felt paralyzed by fear. Her mother's cries were growing louder, and Rachel took the first step into the water. As she waded in slowly, she felt her legs grow heavy. It was difficult to move, as if the water was becoming solid.

Rachel's heart was pounding painfully inside her rib cage. The bright glowing ball appeared near her mother and began circling. She tried to will her legs to move faster, to try to swim out, but she could go no further. She was stuck.

She watched helplessly as another figure appeared, floating toward the center of the lake. *The Lady of the Lake,* Rachel thought. Rachel tried to move with everything she had but could not budge.

The figure approached Kate and slashed at her with her long nails. Rachel screamed, the sound piercing through the night air. She could clearly see the Lady's decayed face and body now, wearing her familiar white robe. She turned and stared at Rachel right in the eyes and moved in her direction. Rachel felt her body go numb with fear.

Rachel's mouth went dry. She should have never entered the lake; she realized that now. It was a trap. She felt powerless as the decaying woman reached her quickly and grabbed her by the neck, tipping her head back and forcing her mouth open. Rachel gagged with terror as the Lady of the Lake brought her mouth close and blew rancid air out. Rachel's body shook, and she collapsed from the terror. The trees began to shake with her, leaves flying into the air. She caught a glimpse of a flashing green light before her eyes rolled back.

She woke with a start. Her head was sinking into the tub, and she pulled herself back up, panting hard. She looked around her bathroom, gaining her bearings, and remembered that she was alone in the house.

"Ouch." Her neck was burning hot. She rose from the tub and felt pain in her legs as she wrapped a towel around herself. Examining her face in the mirror, she noticed red burns on her neck. She touched the burns lightly with her fingertips and quickly pulled her hand back.

The Lady of the Lake, Rachel thought to herself, *what does she want with me?* These weren't just nightmares anymore; they were real.

The front door opened downstairs, and the sound of heels clicking against the wood floor drifted upward. "Christine," Rachel said to herself. She rushed to her wardrobe and grabbed a turtle neck and a skirt, dressing quickly.

She ran down the stairs swiftly to meet her aunt. Christine was warming a meal in the microwave.

"Are you heading out again?" Rachel asked.

"Oh, you're home." She threw a glance at Rachel and returned her gaze to the microwave. "Yeah." She switched off the timer and brought the food out of the microwave. Scooter rushed in as soon as he smelled the food, wagging his tail and circling.

"I'm glad you're home. I want to talk to you about something." Christine's voice was strained. Rachel could sense an issue, and she touched her neck to verify that the shirt covered the marks properly. Christine noticing them would only lead to questions that Rachel could not answer.

"Did you talk with Ben about what we agreed on?" Christine put the meal on the table. Rachel just stared at her, uneasiness brewing in her stomach. The tension was thick in the air, and she could sense that something had happened again with Ben. "No, I haven't had the chance yet."

Christine sighed, shaking her head. "We had an agreement, and you said you were going to talk to him. I'm not happy about this, Rachel. Ben keeps talking about the twins, and I'm trying to act like it's normal. But, unfortunately, he got in trouble again today."

Rachel's eyes widened. "What did he do?"

"The same thing he did last time, took some other kids' food. We're not going to be able to continue like this." Christine locked her eyes on Rachel; Rachel couldn't look her in the eyes. Her throat felt too dry to speak, but she managed.

"I don't know what to say."

Something in Christine's tone alerted Rachel that she wasn't just frustrated by Ben's behavior but the accumulated secrets that left her in the dark. Rachel knew how difficult it was; she wouldn't want to be left out in the same manner.

"Well, they asked me in the principal's office why he isn't in therapy yet," she snapped. "You see the trouble I'm going through?" She paced around the kitchen.

"Where is Ben?" Rachel asked.

"He went upstairs." Christine pointed in the direction of the staircase. "And it's too late to talk to him. He's seeing a mental health professional. And that's final."

"What? But he's not sick!" Rachel insisted.

"What do you want me to do, Rachel? You've seen him talk to empty air, and that's bad enough. Now he's stealing. It's not normal. Besides, the school gave me an ultimatum - suspension, or the therapist. What would you have me choose?" She grabbed her bag and walked off, leaving the food uneaten at the table.

Rachel sat at the table, feeling torn. The Lady of the Lake was winning, and she had no cards up her sleeve.

15

Christine paced back and forth in the waiting room. She wanted a cigarette, an urge she hadn't experienced in years. She glanced over at Ben, sitting in a chair, swinging his legs back and forth. Her heart clenched for him. First, he lost both of his parents, and now this?

The intercom buzzer sounded, and the receptionist nodded at her. "You can go up now. Top floor. The lift is right over there."

The main doors opened as she pivoted towards the elevator, Ben trailing along behind her. A couple of young executives also stood by the lift. Christine gave them a calm smile as she stepped into the cage ahead of them as she turned, aware of their frank appraisal.

The young executives got off on the fifth floor. Continuing to the seventh, Christine and Ben found themselves stepping out onto thick green carpet. There were no directional signs, so she opted for right, clutching Ben's hand beside her. She strolled along the wide corridor past several mahogany doors until they reached the one inscribed with the name she sought.

Hand on the knob, she stood for a long moment gazing at the initials *M.H.* with a sudden tautness in her chest. Ben just stood and watched her. She gently knocked on the door, but there was no response. She knocked again. This time there was a soft voice from inside, saying, "Come in." She stood still and looked down at Ben, who was staring at the floor.

Christine tried to calm her nerves as she turned the knob. She kept telling herself there was no way that whatever was going on with Ben was that serious. He was just a kid. A kid with a traumatic history.

They found themselves in another small waiting room being greeted by a receptionist. She led them back to an inner office, announcing their names. Ornate was Christine's initial evaluation of the large and beautifully furnished room. A floor-to-ceiling, wall-to-wall window afforded a magnificent view out over the city.

The man seated behind the ultra-modern desk had full hair a shade or two darker than her own. Thick and crisply styled, it glinted with health and vitality in the bright sunlight.

"Hello there. I'm glad you guys found your way in; it can be a bit difficult the first time," he mused. "Ms. McAllister, we won't be needing you in this session. It's just going to be me and my man here, Benjamin."

"Ben," Ben corrected, and the therapist nodded with a smile.

Christine took a steadying breath and moved back to the waiting area, shutting the door behind her.

The therapist's dark brows lifted as he registered Ben's composure. He studied him with new interest, eyes open and friendly. Ben let out a breath he didn't know he had been holding. He did not like sitting on a sofa talking to a man he didn't know.

"Hi, Ben. I'm Marshall. You can call me Dr. Marshall, okay?" The therapist stretched out his hand to welcome Ben, and Ben poked his hand out feebly in response.

"Okay," Ben responded.

"I don't know how much you've been told about your visit today, but I'm basically like a doctor for feelings. Just like you go to your regular doctor when you are sick or need a check-up. I've heard that you're having a bit of a rough time at school, and I want to help," Dr. Marshall said warmly.

Ben nodded and continued staring at the floor.

"Okay." Dr. Marshall said. "I also want to tell you that anything you say in here will be confidential. That means everything will be between you and me, and I won't tell your aunt, unless you are in danger. This is a safe space."

Ben nodded and squirmed on the sofa to get more comfortable.

After some general introductory questions, Dr. Marshall moved carefully to the issues at school.

"Can you tell me about your friends at school?" Marshall smiled at Ben encouragingly. He wanted Ben to be able to open up.

"I have some friends that I play with," Ben responded.

"Can you tell me more about them? What are their names?" Dr. Marshall asked.

"I don't want to talk about them," Ben said, looking down at the floor again. "Please, can I have that lollipop?" He pointed to a lollipop in a candy dish next to Dr. Marshall.

"Alright." Marshall took the red lollipop, stretched and handed it to Ben. "How have you been feeling at school? Does going to school feel fun?"

"The twins say you're boring. I want to go, please," Ben said, suddenly disinterested in the situation.

"What twins?" Marshall looked confused.

"My friends, they say you're a bore."

"Are you seeing them right now?" He took off his glasses. His eyes were tiny.

"Yes. I want to go home, please," Ben insisted.

"Okay, we can end the session for the day. I just have one last question today." Marshall was surprised at how unaffected Ben seemed. "How long have you known these twins?"

"Since we were living in Mecklenburg County," Ben replied. "Can I go now?"

"Yes, of course. I'll just have a quick chat with your aunt, and you'll be on your way." He stood up, and Ben followed suit. He opened the office door and signaled for Christine to come in. "Ben, you can wait here. We'll just be a few minutes." Christine was already seated on the same sofa Ben had sat on, eager to learn what Marshall had uncovered.

"That felt fast. What happened?"

"Yes." Marshall made no attempt to offer meaningless condolences. "I think he could still be in some mental shock after what happened to his parents. But, as I said on the phone, children having imaginary friends is not inherently bad and is also not a clear sign of mental illness."

"So, what are you saying, exactly?" Christine asked.

"The death of his parents could have strengthened the relationship he has with his imaginary friends. However,

96

this only becomes an issue because, as you informed me, he is avoiding taking the blame for stealing and using his imaginary friends as a shield." Dr. Marshall said, holding up his palms.

"So, what do you suggest I do?" Christine dropped back heavily onto the sofa, feeling defeated.

"We will dive deeper into this in further sessions. He wanted to end this session early, and I didn't want to push him during our first meeting. I want him to feel comfortable coming here." He put his glasses back on.

"Okay, I'll bring him next week. Thank you very much, Mr. Hanning." She slowly got up and walked to the door.

As they drove home, Christine mulled over the events from the evening. She needed more time to process everything and figure out how to help Ben deal with the stress and trauma he was facing. Ben may not like it, but she was obliged to make sure he was healthy and safe.

"Ben, you know that I love you very much, right? I'm just trying to take care of you the best that I can. You can always come to me if you want to talk about anything." Christine reached her hand back and squeezed his small knee.

"There's nothing wrong with me. I don't want to go back there." Ben finally spoke from the backseat. Christine kept quiet. It was challenging to look at his youthful face and argue. She swallowed the sudden lump in her throat and focused on the road. She was new to parenthood, and things weren't going so smoothly now that Ben was facing suspension.

"We should watch out for Rachel tonight," Ben continued, looking out the window.

"What?" Christine met his eyes in the rearview window, confused. "What's going on with Rachel?"

"It's nothing. My friends just warned that something bad might happen today and that Rachel will be in the middle of it." He turned back to look out of the car window.

Christine shivered. "Something bad might happen? What are you talking about?" She questioned further, but Ben stayed silent.

"Ben, what are you thinking?" she asked.

"Nothing. I'm hungry." He replied.

"Well, it's a good thing we're home now." She parked the car, and they hurried into the apartment.

As Christine prepared dinner, she thought about what Ben had said in the car. Ben and Rachel had been through enough already. They didn't need any more trouble. As far as she was concerned, these invisible twins were not a good influence on her nephew. She hoped and prayed that the therapy would help.

Rachel, curious to hear about Ben's appointment, helped her aunt in the kitchen. She was still resistant to her brother seeing a therapist, but she did want what was best for him. As she set the table, Rachel caught Christine looking at her with a strange expression on her face.

"I'm sorry, Aunt Christine." She apologized sheepishly.

"For what?" Christine looked perplexed.

"For yesterday. I was out of line, and I should have spoken to Ben as I promised." Rachel said.

"Oh, come on, it's okay. Come here." Christine opened her arms and wrapped Rachel in a huge hug. "I love you guys. I know I don't say it much, but I do love you guys."

She squeezed her tighter and kissed her on the forehead. "Off you go, go finish the table."

16

Rachel woke suddenly from her sleep as torrents of rain pounded against her window. She rubbed her eyes and tried to focus on the dark room around her. After a long day, she felt shaky from fatigue. She wrapped herself in her duvet as if it could protect her from her visions of the Lady of the Lake.

She was so tired of the dreams. Focusing on the ceiling above her, she prayed for a restful, dreamless sleep. She silently cursed the Lady of the Lake as her lids grew heavy and her mind succumbed to the memories of Bridge Manor.

As the memories flashed in her mind, she felt overcome with emotion as she believed that everything had happened because of her. She imagined that if she hadn't suffered a concussion from school several years ago, the discussion of going to the summer house for her to recover would never have happened. If it weren't for her, her parents might still be alive.

Tears dripped from her eyes as she pondered the future and the mess she and Ben were in. She wiped them away and tried to focus on sleeping as the storm outside grew fiercer.

Rachel could sense that the Lady of the Lake was going to appear tonight. She almost welcomed it because she was desperate for some answers. How come the Bridge Manor was still tormenting her? Why did her brother still have a connection with the strange twins? Why did her mother keep recurring in her dream? She would get to the bottom of this and was determined not to allow the Lady of the Lake to take control.

She pulled the duvet closer around her neck and traced the mark there. She touched it slowly, rubbing the tips of her fingers against it. She began to wonder if the Lady of the Lake was trying to kill her or possess her.

Her heart began to quicken its pace as her imagination got the better of her. She swallowed and felt a lump in her throat and tried to control her breathing. Her thoughts drifted to her father, how the Lady of the Lake had caused his death. She felt anger rise in her chest, and she was momentarily overwhelmed with the need for revenge.

After a while, Rachel succumbed to deep sleep, and heavy darkness fell over the room. She didn't hear the low growls emanating from the hallway, and she didn't see the large shadow enter her room and tower over her, green eyes shining brightly.

The shadow moved to the window where there was a rumble, and then a bolt of lightning illuminated the room before plunging it back into darkness. Rachel jolted awake and sprang out of bed, alerted to the unknown presence in her room. She could feel that it was the Lady of the Lake.

The shadow was at the other end of the room, eyes glowing brightly. Rachel was momentarily thrown off, expecting an attack, but instead, the shadow exited the room, the door creaking. Rachel breathed out slowly and sank back onto her bed. She squeezed her eyes tightly and tried to figure out her next step. She opened her eyes and gasped in shock because the shadow was there, right above her, mouth open wide. Its gaping hole was full of sharp brown canines and a long, scaled tongue that darted out hungrily.

Rachel shrieked and covered the blanket over her head in fear, but nothing happened. Finally, she heard the creak of the door again and released the blanket. She could see the light in the hallway flickering as the creature moved about. She jumped out of bed and moved to the door, afraid to enter the hallway, afraid to stay in her bedroom.

She steeled herself and peered out the door. The shadow had nearly reached the end of the hallway. Her mind reverted to her time at Bridge Manor, following a shadowy beast through the house and discovering a secret basement. Did Aunt Christine also have an underground basement to uncover? She reminded herself that Bridge Manor had been haunted, and she highly doubted that this apartment building was. She was the one being haunted. She breathed in again slowly, put her hand on her chest, and prayed that no lives would be lost this time.

Tiptoeing into the hallway, she felt her heart spasm in fear and tried to convince herself that this shadowy figure could not hurt her, even if it tried. She would not be passive. She would fight like her life depended on it, because it did. She was not going to let the Lady of the Lake get the better of her.

The shadow continued to growl as it moved downstairs, and although it was a low sound, Rachel wondered if it would wake up Aunt Christine. Rachel followed quietly, keeping her distance, her fear multiplying with every step.

A loud bark cracked through the silence, and Scooter rushed to the bottom of the staircase, barking at the shadow. She glanced upstairs at her aunt's door. Surely she would be awake by now? But as soon as she thought it, the barking stopped. She peered around but couldn't see the shadow anywhere, and Scooter was nowhere in sight. The lights were off downstairs, and she struggled to make out anything in the darkness.

"Scooter, Scooter," she called in a loud whisper. She heard the dog try to respond, but it sounded like it was gasping. In that moment, she realized that she did actually care about the dog.

"Scooter," she called out, loudly this time. She convinced herself she could move a bit further to try and see what was happening. She wasn't going to let the Lady of the Lake make a nervous wreck of her. Her heart sank in fear as she tiptoed deeper into the sitting room, out of reach of the light reflecting from the hallway.

The wind outside banged on the windows and she moved cautiously until her feet collided with something on the floor. She looked around wildly, waving her hands in front of her, afraid of touching something. "Scooter!" she yelled in a panic.

She heard the dog whimper beneath her, and she felt grateful that he was alive. She had never imagined that she would pray for the animal's safety and feel protective over him.

A light in the corner of her eye caught her attention, and she quickly swiveled her head. The shadow's green eyes shined brighter than usual. She ran towards the stairs, and the shadow tried to follow, but it moved slow like it was weighed down. She reached the stairs as the light in the hallway began to flicker, plunging her into darkness for what felt like an eternity before switching back on.

She made it to the door of her bedroom before checking to see if the shadow was behind her. She heard noises down below but couldn't see anything. She breathed a quick sigh of relief, but she knew it wasn't over. Judging from its pace, it wouldn't be long until it reached her. She checked her room to make sure it was safe for her to enter.

Without warning, The Lady of the Lake appeared decaying and terrifying and dragged her into her room by her hair. Rachel flailed wildly, trying to make contact with her foot. Finally, she succeeded and managed to push the Lady of the Lake out into the hallway, slamming the door behind her. She turned the lock with a shaky hand and slumped against the wall. She could hear Scooter barking downstairs. There was no way Aunt Christine could sleep through all of this noise.

Someone, or something, banged on her door from the outside. She rushed into her bathroom and locked the door behind her, praying that the Lady of the Lake would just disappear. She cried as she leaned on the bathroom counter. She didn't want a life full of terror to be her new reality. She wanted to wake up from this nightmare.

She noticed suddenly that the faucet was on in the bathtub. Pulling the curtain back, she saw that the tub was filled to the brim, and as she watched, water began spilling over onto the bathroom floor. She tried to turn the faucet off, but it wouldn't budge. She left it, not wanting to exert her remaining energy.

The water level rose, reaching her ankles. It was rising too quickly, and she grabbed onto the door handle, feeling trapped. Was this some sort of extraordinary performance by the Lady of the Lake? Her heart pounded, and she felt more lucid. She knew that it was time to wake up from this nightmare.

She held the knob tight as the water reached her thigh and tried to force the door open. It was stuck. *It can't be,* she thought to herself. She tried to twist the knob again, but nothing happened. She realized that it was suddenly quiet, save for the rush of running water. She couldn't hear any noises from outside of the door. The bathroom light above her began to flicker, and the water reached her waist. Out of desperation, she moved backward and then kicked the door handle as hard as she could. It didn't budge. She tried over and over again, but her only escape remained shut tight. Tears streamed down her cheeks, a mixture of terror and exhaustion. Was this how it all ended?

The water continued to rise until a bright ball of light burst out of the tub and illuminated the bathroom. Rachel's tears ceased as she watched the light, peering into the tub, trying to figure out where it had come from. As she watched in horror, a hand reached out slowly from the tub, beckoning her in. Rachel's heart was pounding as she examined the hand. Was it the Lady of the Lake?

She tried the door one last time, pulling and shoving in desperation. Boom. Water filled the small bathroom at an alarming rate. She was sinking. She tried to raise her head out of the water, but it was as if she was being pulled down. She let out a scream of frustration, but the water muffled the sound. She struggled to come up for air, but it was too late. She lost the strength to resist and was forced to accept her fate.

The sunlight peeking through Christine's windows woke her. She walked to the bathroom in a sleepy haze and splashed water on her face. Then she crawled back in bed. It was the weekend, and she didn't need to worry about going to the art gallery. She thought about dinner with the kids the night before. It had been pleasant. Slowly but surely, through everything, they were becoming a family.

She hopped out of bed and donned her robe and slippers to check on Ben. Yesterday had been a big day for him, and she was concerned. His behavior worried her.

Christine opened the door and headed to Ben's room, only to stop because her feet were wet. She saw that water was seeping under Rachel's door, out into the hallway.

"What in the world—." She grabbed the handle and turned, but it was locked. She banged on the door.

"Rachel, are you okay? Open the door." She banged harder, but there was no response.

Frantic now, she turned the handle with all of her strength. The door flew open and more water gushed out into the hallway.

"Rachel!" she yelled. The room was empty. She rushed to the bathroom and opened the door. The faucet was running in the tub, and water was spilling out. *Rachel is so dead*, she thought to herself.

"Rachel?" she called out again loudly. She made her way over to the tub and shut off the faucet, stopping the flow of water.

Where on earth was Rachel.

She made her way downstairs, calling Rachel's name. She checked the sitting room, but it was empty. She was turning to leave when she noticed a stain on the rug. Was that blood? Her heartbeat quickened, and she rushed to the kitchen. She gasped and dropped to the floor in horror. There was Scooter, lifeless on the floor, blood spilling from his throat. Christine made it to the sink and retched, horrified at the scene in front of her. Who would have done this?

She had to find the kids.

"Ben?" There was no reply. "Ben!" she screamed, running back upstairs. She couldn't lose all three of them in one day. She threw open the door to Ben's room, gasping for breath. The bed was empty.

"I'm here, auntie." Ben finally answered from under the bed.

"Oh love, thank God. Why are you hiding under the bed?" Christine knelt down and stretched out her hand to pull him out.

"I'm scared," he said as he slowly crawled out. "I'm scared. I don't want to be taken away."

"Taken away?" Christine questioned. "No one is taking you away. I'm here. No one is going to take you away from your sister or me, alright." Ben nodded and hugged her tightly. Christine frowned. What the hell had happened last night?

"Okay, Ben. Now tell me, where is your sister?"

He took a deep breath, held it for a moment before letting it out and speaking in a rush.

"Rachel is gone."

"What do you mean Rachel is gone. Where did she go? It's okay, Ben, you can tell me." She hugged him to her.

"She's been taken. She's been taken by The Lady of the Lake."

III

THE LADY OF THE LAKE

17

MECKLENBURG COUNTY, 1869

A gentle breeze greeted all who walked across the long, manicured lawn leading to the Bridge Manor. A long queue waited outside, right up to the front porch. Then, one by one, they raised their invites to the man guarding the front door and entered the Manor. The night air was ripe with energy. Music and excited chatter spilled out from the grand house. Everyone wanted a taste of the Madeira wine; it was Michael Bridge's favorite. He frequented a pub near the lake to drink it every afternoon, and the people of Mecklenburg County gradually began to crave the wine because Bridge enjoyed it. The wine had a dry, spicy aroma that lingered on the glass, a multi-layered fruitiness that encouraged you to take another sip.

The merriment and dancing continued, and the crowd cheered as Bridge tapped his wine glass for attention. Then, he gestured grandly to the staircase as his wife and the twins made their entrance.

"Ladies and gentlemen, I present to you my family."
The majority of the crowd clapped and cheered, and the
noise reverberated around the room.

Catherine Bridge was a vision in a full skirt and fitted
bodice fashioned from light-weight sheer wool. An
elaborate lace collar floated over her shoulders. A sense of
awe hushed the crowd.

As she proceeded leisurely down the stairs, the crowd
parted. Michael Bridge stood tall and proud, eyes fixed on
his wife. A small smile tugged at the corners of his lips. He
raised his hands to the air and began to speak.

"For three years, I proudly served this country," he
began. "I couldn't make heads or tails of where my life was
going to go. But I knew one thing, I was going to fight with
everything I had in me. And I did just that, and though we
didn't win, I survived to make my mark differently. So we
are going to make history here, and tonight marks the
beginning."

The crowd cheered, and some began to sing victory
songs. Although the rest of the group did not understand
the lyrics, they chanted on.

As the night progressed and the moon grew higher in
the sky, the din from the manor attracted more of the
townspeople. They trooped en masse to the front door,
demanding entry. Bridge ordered the doors shut to the
new visitors and then departed to the basement with a
couple of men, the Sheriff and the Mayor included.

Planks lined the walkway into the basement, as the
stairway was partly damaged. "Be careful," Bridge warned.
"The masons did a poor job with the stairway, and I noticed
it late." They walked down carefully; the room was mostly
empty except for the tools and remnants of wood used in

the building. A table stood at the center of the room fashioned from a quarter-sawn oak tree. Bridge, with an eye for design, had specifically chosen the Irish craftsmen who handcrafted the wood.

"Gentlemen, you all know why you are here?" Bridge coughed as they circled the table. Bridge, the Sheriff, the Mayor, and his secretary each took their seats while the others crowded around them.

"There is a written agreement as to the money which is to be accrued for pulling strings so that you may own this land." The Mayor looked at Bridge, then continued.

"The Sheriff will ensure you don't get harassed by the townspeople. You know there are angry people, Bridge, who didn't want you to acquire this land. Even men here."

Bridge looked around at the men in the room, and they returned his gaze with stony expressions. Finally, he forced a smile and said, "I appreciate everything you have done for my family and me. I am grateful and will do anything necessary not to destroy the good work you have dedicated."

The Sheriff retrieved a scroll from the pocket of his brown leather coat. "You have to sign here, sir." He pointed to the spot, "The document says you'll pay 2000 dollars annually for five years."

Michael Bridge hesitated, his pen hovering over the paper. Two thousand was an unreasonable fee to keep their mouths shut. However, it was public land - he knew he had no right to it. He swallowed, uncomfortable seeing that all eyes were focused on him. He knew the situation could escalate if he failed to adhere to the demands.

"Is this negotiable?" Bridge tried, knowing that it was already too late to haggle the price. Receiving no response, his eyes ran across their unflinching faces one more time. The room was tense, and he felt like he couldn't maneuver his way through this. Michael Bridge signed.

"Well done," the Sheriff said, tapping him on the back. Bridge pushed his body away slightly to indicate his displeasure.

A loud bang alerted the men as the basement door flew open. Noise spilled into the room from the party above, and a man came tumbling down the staircase. He landed in front of them, his body hitting the floor with a thud. They all rushed to his aid.

"Apologies, the stairway needs to be repaired." Bridge knelt to help the man.

"What's going on? Why did you barge in like that?" the Sheriff inquired.

"Can you hear all that noise up there?"

"Yes. What's the issue?" The Sheriff was growing impatient.

"Locals are protesting outside and are trying to force their way through. They've already started a small fire, but we managed to put it out." Bridge felt panic rising in his chest, and the atmosphere became saturated with confusion. Finally, the Sheriff and his men ran upstairs to control the situation.

"Don't worry, they'll have it quickly under control," the Mayor assured Bridge.

As soon as the words left the Mayor's lips, the Sheriff rushed down the stairs and shouted, "I think you all should come to see this for yourselves."

The dark sky roared as Bridge stepped outside to join the Sheriff and his men. Hundreds of wood-laden torches were wielded by an angry mob, roaring in protest against the manor's grand opening.

"You're bringing a curse upon this county!" a man yelled from the mob.

"We won't let this happen!" shouted another. "Burn it to the ground!"

Bridge raised his hands, a gesture to call for calm amongst the locals. But, as he attempted to manage the crowd, a large black gooey substance flew past him and hit the Sheriff in his face.

"Eat horseshit, you dogs," a man shouted from the crowd, and the people cheered him on wildly. Others gained courage and began throwing tomatoes at them. Some threw stones in an attempt to shatter the glass windows.

"We're not going to stand here and take this shit from these fools." The Sheriff snorted and cocked his gun. He pointed it into the crowd and yelled some angry words at them. They retreated slightly but didn't stop throwing tomatoes.

"You want to try me, aye?" He scowled angrily. His eyes were bloodshot, and his face was red. "Try me and see!" he roared louder. He waved the gun at the crowd, and they pushed back a little more. Another tomato flew through the crowd and landed at his feet. He pulled the trigger and fired into the air, and finally, the crowd dispersed, running in all directions.

"Get out of here, you scoundrels!" The heat was on.

The Mayor tapped Bridge on his shoulder. "There will always be those who want to take down people in powerful positions. But you have powerful friends on your side. We'll stop these scoundrels from disturbing you and your family. You have my word."

The Mayor and his men retreated into the house, where the party was on pause. Bridge remained outside, facing the house. Above the wooden lintel was a slab with the inscription BRIDGE MANOR. He read the words and smiled, then followed the men inside.

The party-goers slowly trickled out, thanking them for a lovely evening, despite the commotion.

As Bridge fell into a restless sleep that night, his thoughts circled to the angry crowd intent on making sure his dreams were never fulfilled. He believed that the resentment building inside of them would lead them to go to any lengths to trespass and cause havoc in his life.

As the chants in his head increased, he could no longer tell if they were purely inside of his head or if they were real. Finally, growing irritated, he leaped from the bed and yelled out the window, "Who's there?" He reached for the drawer beside his bed and grabbed his handgun.

Bridge was known for being a bit mad and was certainly not the type of man worth messing with. He exited from the front door and rushed onto the patio. Surveying his land, he searched for the trespassers. He spotted them, three people, dressed in black with black hats.

"Stop right there, you scoundrels." He shouted and waved his gun wildly at them. They chuckled and quickly vanished into thin air before his eyes.

Bridge rubbed his eyes in disbelief. Where did they get off to? He turned to descend the porch steps when he tripped and fell over something.

"What in the—?" He marveled at the object at his feet, a heavy leather-bound book.

"For Michael Bridge," Bridge read, a surge of resentment and irritation built in his veins. He took a seat on the porch bench, clouded in confusion, and attempted to uncover the meaning behind this mysterious delivery.

18

"For goodness' sake, Ben, get out of bed and get dressed. We need to head to the station."

Ben stood up from the bed slowly and wiped his eyes. Christine stalked the hallway, tense. She was breathing hard, her right hand placed on her head. Beads of sweat formed on her forehead; Rachel's disappearance was wearing her down. Usually calm, Christine was in a panic over the whereabouts of her niece.

"I've been trying to reach the police, but they won't take the report over the phone. So we have to go there in person. Hurry up, Ben. We need to find your sister." She peered into his room.

Ben had barely moved and was still in his pajamas. Christine stopped outside the door and collapsed, her face in her hands. How did Rachel slip away from her? Was it her absent-mindedness that blinded her from the obvious? Christine found that she couldn't move, as if she was being held motionless by these thoughts. The girl she had believed she could protect had slipped away.

"Aunt Christine, I'm sorry," Ben called out timidly. Christine wiped the tears away and looked at him.

"Oh, Ben. It's not your fault."

"I mean, I wet the bed."

Christine sighed.

"It's okay, dear. This is scary for all of us. Let's get you cleaned up and get out of here. We need to find Rachel."

Christine's heartbeat drummed in her ears, muscles tensing as she drove to the police station. She turned to the side to glance at Ben, who was sitting in the passenger's seat. He appeared unperturbed, his eyes focused on the road. Christine was perplexed at how he retained such calm. Strange but not strange, Christine witnessed this silence after his parents' death. She wanted to ask him again where he thought Rachel might be, but she already knew his answer. It made him sound delusional. *"She's been taken by The Lady of the Lake."* His words echoed in her head.

Ben shook his hair out of his eyes, long overdue for a haircut, jeans a bit faded, his shirt frayed at the collar. His external appearance belied his mental state, Christine thought. How was she already failing both Rachel and Ben as a guardian?

"It just isn't right for your sister to leave like that." Christine blurted out, hoping to gain new information from Ben. But Ben sat quietly and kept his gaze on the road.

"You don't want to talk about it anymore?" Christine questioned, but clearly, he didn't want to talk. Ben looked troubled, his expression cold.

They reached their destination at eight-thirty to find a desk sergeant sitting at the desk. Youngish and muscle-bound, he gave Christine a once-over as she approached. His cheeky smile exposed his dimples. "What can I do for you, ma'am?"

"My ward has been missing since either late last night or early this morning. We need to find her now." Christine wasn't interested in chatting or niceties. Instead, she steeled her arm on the table and tried to lean over to grab a form.

"Please, calm down, ma'am." The desk sergeant pushed her hand back gently. "I know you're upset and worried, but let's take this one step at a time." He flipped open his notebook and clicked his pen.

"Okay. Who is missing?"

"Rachel McAllister." Christine burst into tears as she said the name. Nevertheless, she was grateful that the police understood the urgency of the case.

"It's okay, ma'am." He tried to console her and offered her a cup of coffee which she turned away.

"How old is she?"

"Only sixteen." Christine sniffed.

"Do you need some tissues?" the desk sergeant asked, offering her a box of Kleenex.

"Yes, thank you."

"Is that your son?" he asked, gesturing at Ben. She looked down at Ben, his overgrown hair partially covering his face.

"No, he's my ward," she said, finally finding her voice.

"And the missing girl is also your ward?"

"Yes."

"How long has she been missing? You're not sure if it was last night or this morning?"

Her mouth opened and closed. She had never considered this scenario in her life; she felt numb. The mere thought of Rachel missing was enough to make her weak.

"You can take your time." The desk sergeant had soothing words. Christine's face felt hot.

"Cases like this are common. So it's best to keep calm and collected so we can gather all the details we can."

Tears trickled down her face, but she didn't seem to notice.

"How long has she been missing, ma'am?" He threw a glance at Ben, but Ben just stared straight ahead.

"We had dinner together last night, and everything seemed normal. But I woke up this morning to find my dog dead in the kitchen and water leaking out from her room, and she wasn't there." Her nose began dripping again.

"Okay, let's back up a bit. Was your house burgled?"

"No. I checked, but nothing was missing in the house except her."

The desk sergeant leaned back in his chair and looked like he was trying to find the right words for what he wanted to say. Then, clearing his throat, he asked, "Is it possible that Rachel ran away? It's not uncommon for teens to run away, especially if something was going on at home."

Christine looked aghast. "Rachel wouldn't run away. We have an excellent relationship. She's missing. Something has happened to her!"

The desk sergeant nodded, continued asking questions and taking notes until he seemed satisfied. "I'll finish up the report now. It's best if you go home and wait for her to return."

Christine covered her face with her hands and tried not to let her thoughts overrun her. She felt like she was stuck in a terrible nightmare and couldn't wake up.

Christine used the rearview mirror to check for oncoming cars. Excruciating pain pounded through her head, and she could hardly focus. She was not heading straight home; she had an important stop to make first.

She rolled down the windows, hoping that the fresh air would help clear her head. The cool air felt good on her skin as they drove down the road in silence. She didn't know what to talk about with Ben. Her thoughts kept drifting to Rachel, and she didn't know what to think. There was no sign of a break-in. Did Rachel run away? What was she running away from? Why was her dog dead?

When Christine rounded the corner and pulled into the parking lot, she was surprised to see Ben's therapist, Marshall Hanning, in what appeared to be an argument with another man. Marshall was shaking his head, his right hand slicing the air.

"I don't know how you could come here and say it," the therapist spat. "After all, what's so terrible about—." He stopped dead in his tracks.

"Hello, Miss McAllister, how are you?" He sounded surprised to see her.

His weather-beaten face was thinner and sharper than usual, blue eyes blazing.

"We need to talk. It's urgent." She said, gripping Ben's hand tightly.

"Let's go upstairs." He pointed towards the glass door, gesturing that they should enter. "We'll finish this later." He told the man before following Christine and Ben inside.

They made their way through the office building up to the top floor. This time she noticed elaborate landscapes hanging on the walls. As they walked, Marshall inquired about Rachel. Christine's heart felt like it was going to beat out of her chest. *How did he know?*

"Why do you ask about Rachel?" Christine tried to keep her voice even.

"No reason. I just thought she might have some experience with trauma herself since she and Ben are going through this traumatic event."

"Of course." She tried to steady her heartbeat, figuring his line of questioning was reasonable. They walked past his secretary and into his office.

"The pinnacle of every traumatizing event is hinged on the fact that others share the same experience," he said warmly. "I'm only asking to help." A smile tugged on his face. "Please, sit down." He pointed to the sofa, and Christine and Ben sat.

"Now, what is so urgent, Miss McAllister?" Then, lifting a large file full of papers, he idly began to flip through them with a pretense of curiosity.

"Rachel is missing."

The therapist shut the file, a look of surprise on his face. "Missing? What do you mean?"

"I woke up this morning, and Rachel had vanished, and my dog was lying dead in the kitchen," Christine said in a rush, a tone of numbness in her voice.

"This sounds serious. Have you gone to the police?"

"They took down a report, but I don't feel like they're taking it very seriously. They think she's a runaway." Anger tightened her features. Christine saw Marshall's face soften. "Maybe I didn't realize that Rachel needed more attention. I've been focusing more on Ben, and perhaps something was going on, and she didn't want to talk to me about it." She buried her face in her hands, muffling a sob.

"There, there. We're always just doing the best we can." Marshall reassured her. Then he turned his attention to Ben.

"How are you feeling, Ben? This must be quite a shock, waking up to find your sister missing."

Ben didn't look up.

"Ben?" Marshall tried again. "Has Rachel said anything to you? Was something going on?"

"She's not dead. The Lady of the Lake took her." Ben continued looking down, staring at his hands.

"What?" The therapist looked confused. He leaned forward, curiosity piqued. "Who is the Lady of the Lake?"

Christine felt like the rest of the day passed in a blur. She could barely remember much of their conversation at the therapist's office. Ben didn't talk much after his declaration. It was a quiet, restless evening at the McAllister's.

Christine decided that Ben should sleep with her in her room, scared to think of what might happen to him in the night if she let him out of her gaze. Wrapped in a small blanket, Christine laid Ben next to her. Her mind wandered as he drifted off. She had spent most of the day pacing the house, listening for the phone, praying that Rachel would come home. Her heart ached with worry. Then, just as she was dozing off, she heard a faint buzzing sound. Was it in her dream? She jerked up and slipped off of the bed, running out into the hallway, hunting down the noise. It was coming from Rachel's room.

She stood at Rachel's door and took a deep breath. Her body felt heavy and cold. She pushed the door open and grabbed the phone, lighting up and vibrating on the nightstand. 'Unknown Caller' flashed across the screen.

"Hello?" Christine breathed softly.

Ben stood in Rachel's doorway and watched as his aunt answered the phone. Christine's expression changed from fear to hope to disbelief. The phone slipped from her hand and crashed onto the floor as she collapsed, sobbing, onto the bed.

19

MECKLENBURG COUNTY

"**H**ELP!"
The calls were falling deaf in the night.
The neighborhood was still and sleepy,
Rachel's desperate pleas for help the only sound. The wind
and the trees swallowed her cries. She didn't know how
she ended up here, but she knew exactly where she was.

She alternated between calling for help and using her
energy to attempt to fight off the force holding her in the
lake. She floated aimlessly, unable to pull her body out of
the murky water, trapped on the surface. She attempted to
grab onto the weed grass and pull herself out, but it was
futile.

"Please stop." She cried out, testing every inch of her
patience as she struggled to break free. She was gradually
losing touch with reality, her mind slowly fading away.

A glowing ball appeared, hovering above the lake,
pulsing brightly. She tried to focus on it but could feel
herself fading away. As she watched, her mother and the
Lady of the Lake appeared, gliding towards her. Her eyes

widened as she recognized her mother's pale face. Tiny shards of recollection pieced together in her head, memories of the long night flooded her vision. Flashes of her mother stained with her father's blood. Then, with her last bit of strength, she let out a final cry, her body sinking under the surface as she passed out.

Kenneth didn't know what woke him up. The night was eerily silent as he tossed and turned, trying to fall back asleep. Finally, giving up, he walked to his window and peered out into the night, and then stumbled back in shock. A woman was floating on the surface of the lake. Kenneth had seen the Lady of the Lake before, but something about this scene was different. He knew this was not the ghostly woman. Who was there? Was someone out for a swim? No, it was far too late for that.

"Dad!" He called out, hoping to wake him up.

There was no response. He felt drawn to the lake. He pulled on a shirt and rushed out of the house, running towards the lake. As he drew nearer, he could see the woman bobbing back and forth. She was definitely not swimming. She needed help.

At the lake's edge, his feet touched the water first, and he was surprised to feel that the water was warm. It lapped over his cold feet as he made his way further into the lake. Swimming now, he sped up, feeling that time was of the essence. Then, less than ten feet away, he experienced a gut-wrenching, sharp spasm in his leg. He shouted aloud in shock and pain.

He tried to pull himself to continue, but something had caught onto his leg. He couldn't go further. Thinking of his father back at the house, he opened his mouth to call out and shut it again. His father would probably be furious with him for investigating this scenario in the middle of the night, alone.

Don't panic, he told himself, but his body was refusing to obey him. And the more the leg stiffened, the more the woman began to sink beneath the surface. He reached down to try and free his leg, but nothing appeared to be entrapping him.

Fear overwhelmed Kenneth, and the panic caused him to lose consciousness momentarily. As his eyes snapped back open, he found that the woman had nearly disappeared below the water. At last, his leg was free, and he closed the distance between them.

"Misses!" It still wasn't clear to him who he was going to save. "For God's sake, please stay alive. I'm almost there!"

Rachel could barely hear the voice calling out to her. She had gone deep into her subconscious. Slowly, she was slipping deeper and deeper, choking as the water swallowed her.

"Rachel?!"

At first, Kenneth was stunned. Then, he quickly grabbed hold of her, hauled her from beneath the surface, and threw her over his shoulder as best he could. He swam quickly back to the shore and then slapped the flat of his palm hard between her shoulder blades, and she spat and retched water, sobbing with relief as she hugged him.

"Easy now," he soothed. "Easy." He ran his hands experimentally down her legs until he found out her legs were stiffened and cramped.

"Ouch!" she gasped.

Rachel had little memory of what brought her into Mecklenburg County. Instead, she remembered sinking into the bathtub at her Aunt Christine's house as a strange hand pulled her beneath. First, Rachel felt the relief of spewing up water from her lungs and breathing in the cool night air. And then Kenneth was rubbing her legs between his hands until the spasms ebbed away.

She must have passed out again, for when she came to, she found herself on a bed, the fine, white sheets sticking to her skin, surrounded by soft pillows.

"You're okay," Kenneth murmured reassuringly.

She coughed, then nodded, a sob forming in her throat as she thought about just how lucky she had been.

He felt her shudder. "Don't cry. It's okay now. You're alive."

She tried to get up but couldn't move. She felt as if her limbs had been weighted with lead.

"I don't know what's happening... how did I get here?" She choked.

"Well, we don't know that either. I just found you out in the lake," he told her gently. "It was certainly strange, but you're here now."

She closed her eyes, and the memories began to rush back. She tightened up in fear, and Kenneth rose to his feet to hold her.

She regained herself and slumped to the bed. "We have trouble on our hands." She paused. "Or should I say, I have trouble on my hands?" She pushed a damp lock of hair back from her face, and even that seemed to take every bit of strength she had. Her escape from death had weakened her.

"What trouble? What do you mean?" Kenneth asked curiously.

Rachel's mind felt sluggish, and she tried to get it working again. She sat up slightly. "You remember I told you about these strange dreams I've been having?"

Kenneth nodded.

"Well, they aren't just dreams. I don't know how to place them, but I know I'm always active physically in those dreams. I think the Lady of the Lake wants me dead."

"What?" Kenneth was alarmed by her revelation. "I know this is going to sound strange coming from me, but you just might be suffering from traumatic stress."

There was an odd, brittle pause. "You of all people shouldn't say that," she whispered back, thinking how inadequate his words were because of what he had seen and experienced.

"We burned down the house; there shouldn't be any connection anymore. The spell should be broken." Kenneth looked at her, his eyes narrowing.

She heard the element of fear and caution that had crept into his voice. "Then explain to me how I got here." Her voice was low and tired.

"You should get some rest. Then, in the morning, we can discuss this more." He gave her arm a tiny squeeze and headed for the sitting room to get some sleep.

Rachel scrambled quickly out of bed as the memories of last night came flooding back to her. She realized that she should call her aunt first thing, knowing that she must be worried sick. Then, she walked to the kitchen and saw Kenneth's father making omelets.

"Good morning, Rachel." He seemed agitated and excited. He flipped the omelet inside the frying pan and hurriedly grabbed a plate.

"Mr. Patterson, good morning." She pecked him on the cheek as soon as he dropped the eggs onto the plate. "I'm sure Kenneth already filled you in on everything."

He nodded, and they both sat at the small dining table to catch up. Mr. Patterson was curious and wanted to know more about the events of the previous night. As they talked, Kenneth joined them in the kitchen. "Rachel." Kenneth greeted her warmly.

"Would it be possible to use your phone?" Rachel asked. "I need to call my aunt. She must be so worried about me."

"Actually," Kenneth looked sheepish, "I've already talked to her. I called your phone last night, and she answered. I figured she would be worried about you."

Rachel looked relieved that she didn't have to make the call herself and face more questioning from her aunt.

"Rachel," Kenneth continued. "I don't know how to tell you this, but your aunt said that you'd already been missing for an entire day. Around 24 hours had passed before I found you. Do you know where you were?"

Rachel shook her head, confused. "No, I don't remember anything. I was at my aunt's house in the bathroom and then you were rescuing me from the lake."

Mr. Patterson cleared his throat. He was clearly waiting for more information from Rachel on what exactly brought her to Mecklenburg County.

Her eyebrows rose. "Yes, Mr. Patterson?"

"So, what do you think is going on? How are you here?" he asked slowly, staring at Rachel with concern in his eyes.

"I haven't been doing well. I explained some of it to you guys when you called me recently." Rachel met his probing gaze. "The Lady of the Lake continues to torment me in my dreams, and yesterday, she brought me here."

"She what? How could she do that?" Mr. Patterson looked confused.

Rachel grimaced and shook her head. "I often have nightmares about my mother and the Lady of the Lake. In some nightmares, the Lady of the Lake attacks my mother, and in some, they both attack me. I don't know what this means, but I know she is out there to haunt me. Sometimes I just wish my parents hadn't come here in the first place. I wish that they had never bought this house." She paused. "Yesterday, it was raining, and then she came to me in the form of a shadow. I know I wasn't dreaming this time. Plus, she killed my aunt's dog, Scooter. I ran to my bathroom to hide, but I was trapped. The whole room filled with water, and the Lady of the Lake dragged me under. And somehow, she brought me out here."

"She obviously wants something with you, but what is it?" Mr. Patterson questioned. "If she wanted to kill you, wouldn't she have done it already?"

"Maybe she doesn't want you dead because there's something she wants you to do for her," Kenneth suggested.

"But wouldn't that be clear by now? Why drag it out for so long?" Patterson dismissed the theory.

"What do you think, Mr. Patterson?" Rachel was relieved that she could talk to people about the issue now, people who would believe her.

"We have to do more investigating and find out for ourselves."

"I don't know how long I'm going to be here." Her voice trailed off, and she sounded exasperated. Kenneth and his father glanced at her.

Immediately, she slumped to the floor. Kenneth and his father rushed to her aid, her body shaking vigorously. Her skin suddenly turned pale, and her mouth began oozing out foam.

"Turn her on her side." Patterson barked at his son. Kenneth rushed to comply, his hands trembling.

"C'mon, Kenneth!" He tugged on him to push her on her side, and Kenneth leaned her on her shoulder. Just then, her eyes suddenly opened, and they both stumbled back in shock as green flashed from Rachel's eye sockets. Her body began to shake harder, and they couldn't contain her. She thrashed about, unusually strong.

"What do you think is wrong with her?" Kenneth began to cry.

"I don't know, son." Patterson threw a glance at him. "But we are certain of one thing, the Lady of the Lake is responsible for this. We have to stop her!"

"We have to. We have to save Rachel!" Kenneth echoed.

20

MECKLENBURG COUNTY, 1869

Reverend Tobey was known for two things: being unusually tall and possessing great skill in casting out demons. The last three exorcisms he conducted were in New York, Connecticut, and Missouri, respectively. He was often called in to different towns, and he was not often honored in his town, Mecklenburg County. Despite administering the Church's sacraments with care and visiting the sick, the townspeople did not appear to have great respect for the man.

Catherine awaited Tobey's arrival, sitting up straighter in her chair and jumping as her husband flung open the door.

"He'll be here shortly. Are you ready for this?" Bridge asked, stony-faced.

"It's better we do it." She smiled at him uncertainly. Her face was pale, and she had dark splotches under her eyes. Her lips were dry like a worn-out fabric, and her bones were protruding through her skin. "It is for the children. For the betterment of our children," she whispered feebly before turning to look at the twins standing at the entrance door.

"Hi, darlings. Are you two comfortable?" She smiled at them. Tears filled their eyes at seeing their mother in such a state.

"It's a shame we have to see you like this, love." Michael Bridge dropped onto the middle cushion of the sofa, facing her. She tried to move her hand to reach out to him but struggled against the rope tying her down. He reached out instead, keeping his distance but touching the tips of her fingers with his. "I love you, we love you." He looked back at the twins, and they echoed, "We love you, mummy."

"I love you too, my babies." She smiled, but it turned into a grimace.

"Off to your room, you two. Reverend Tobey will be arriving shortly," he announced.

They scrambled off quickly, and four men walked in as they left.

"Who are these men, Michael?" She looked at him with fear in her eyes.

"These men are here in case the demon chooses to manifest. You know I can't handle it alone." A terrible wail pierced the room as Catherine tried to break free, tugging on the rope with her wrists, to no avail. "Stop that," Bridge said sharply.

"I want to hold my babies!" she screamed.

"You are only going to scare them. Stay put, Catherine."

"Oh, I had completely forgotten." She laughed maniacally. "I forgot that I'm not a parent, that a parent is not a parent, and irrespective of their condition, they still love them unconditionally," she retorted.

"Let's leave the room." Bridge signaled the men to follow him.

Catherine yelled and struggled to break free as they left. Then she laughed and screamed, "I'm coming for you, Michael. I'm coming for all of you!"

The four men walked down the stairs while Bridge walked to his daughters' room. They were eight years old, Emily and Yvonne. "My babies." Bridge teased them as he gently opened the door to their room.

"Daddy!" they both exclaimed and hurriedly hugged him.

"My babies," he said again, but this time a kiss on their forehead accompanied it.

"I just want you both to know that whatever happens, Daddy is going to be here for you." He smiled and squeezed them tighter.

"Is mummy going to be like this forever?" Tears formed in Emily's eyes.

"I don't know, honey. I'm not certain about that." He rubbed her hair gently.

"Are we going to be possessed too?"

"No, honey. Don't ever think that, okay?" His palm cupped her tiny face softly. She nodded.

"That's my little girl." He kissed both on the forehead and bade them goodnight.

The knock on the front door prompted the four men to stand up. Bridge walked to the door and opened it to find himself face to face with Tobey, dressed in his surplice and purple stole. There was no small talk or exchange of pleasantries. He was there for a job, and he was going to execute it.

Tobey had arrived promptly, just as the sun was sinking below the horizon. He was well over six feet tall, with dark hair cut short and sprinkled with gray at the temples, gray eyes in a sharply hewn face. He held an air of sophistication around him, but all Bridge cared about was that he would be able to perform this mission successfully.

The four men were Tobey's assistants, and they accompanied him on every exorcism. He usually sent them ahead to gain a feel for the situation before he arrived.

"Is there somewhere we can talk?" Tobey spoke with a baritone voice.

"Yes, right this way, father." Bridge pointed in the direction of the sitting room as he locked the front door behind him. "Your assistants are already seated."

"Gentlemen," Tobey said, and immediately the four men circled him. It was a strange sight for Bridge; he walked slowly to an armchair and sat, hands resting lightly on his lap.

The men conversed in a low tone, leaving Michael Bridge in the dark. Bridge strained his ears to listen but could not make out what they were saying. It was probably for the best, as he did not want to disrespect the man.

They broke free from the circle and turned to face Bridge.

"We are going to ask you some questions about your wife and what you have observed recently. So please, we want you to be as sincere as possible," the priest said.

Bridge nodded in agreement.

"When would you say you noticed that something was off?"

Bridge sighed heavily. "I can't say for certain when the whole thing started; my wife was the same for a long time. We've been married for fifteen years, and it took time for us to have kids. But throughout our marriage, she never showed any sign of mental illness."

"I'd like you to pinpoint the moment you noticed she appeared to be possessed." Tobey's voice was calm, inquisitive.

"She started behaving strangely around two months ago. She would become suddenly aggressive, and I began to fear for the children's safety. The first time I had to pin her down, I noticed that her eyes flashed green. She possessed more physical strength than she would ordinarily. It was then that I realized this wasn't ordinary." He breathed out heavily as he said the last words.

Tobey took some notes and then stood up slowly and walked to the center of the sitting room. "We are going to perform an exorcism. We are going to cast the evil spirit out of your beloved."

Michael Bridge sighed in relief.

The priest moved slowly around the room. "I can feel the power of God. Michael, you'll have to bring your wife here. We shall perform the exorcism here in the sitting room."

Bridge opened his mouth to speak, but the priest placed his index finger in the air, signaling for him to keep quiet.

"Father, it's the children. Are they going to be okay here in the house? They are too young to experience a thing like this." Bridge's face turned red with worry. The priest looked at him, unconcerned.

"These demons do not know who is young and who is not, they see a host, and they possess. It's that simple." He was calm and yet so convincing. "You let the evil spirit loose, and it's going to torment you and your family, not just Catherine. So let me handle the situation." He placed a hand on Bridge's shoulder, giving him the assurance he needed. He nodded, feeling strangely bereft.

Catherine was seated at the center of the living room. She felt helpless, but even in her demoralized state, she recognized that it was for the good of her family.

"Michael?" she called weakly.

He looked down at her, forgetting that she was possessed, getting lost in those brown eyes of hers. Then, a flash of green dashed those thoughts away. "Yes, what is it?"

"What is happening? Will I be okay?" She cried.

"Yes, you will," he assured her.

"Thank you," she whispered, thinking how inadequate those two words were considering what he was doing for her.

Tobey entered the room, and his deft fingers clenched the Bible in his hand. His assistants followed him and spread out in the room. All eyes were open wide in anticipation, waiting for the father to perform a miracle. He took his place in front of Catherine and opened the Bible.

"I will now recite a series of prayers and appeals." Tobey cleared his throat and began the recitation, asking God to free Catherine from the devil.

An assistant provided Tobey with holy water, and he began to sprinkle it on the participants in the room. As he approached Catherine, her pale face came alive. Her eyes shined bright with green, and she struggled against the ropes. The air was soon filled with her tormented cries.

"Mummy," one of the twins screamed. They all turned in the direction of the staircase and saw the twins standing there.

"Go back to your room!" Bridge barked at his children. He ran towards the staircase, and they scrambled back upstairs, crying.

Tobey sprinkled the holy water on Catherine and re-opened the Bible to recommence his recitation.

"Tonight, we are expelling an unknown demon. We have Christ and His Word, and all things are made possible through him," Tobey recited.

Bridge wasn't sure what to make of this situation. On the one hand, he went to Church every Sunday with his family, but on the other hand he didn't know if he believed that one could be possessed by the devil. He was upset seeing his wife bound to a chair in such a state, but he didn't know what else to do at this point. He had already tried everything.

Refocusing on the ritual at hand, he followed the priest's words.

"Matthew chapter 8 verse 28." The priest paused and took a breath. "And when he came to the other side into the country of Gergesenes, there he met two people possessed by the devil. Just like your wife here." He glanced at Catherine and then continued reading. "And, behold, they cried out, what have we done to thee. What have we to do with thee, Jesus, son of God?"

"They were afraid of Jesus, so we will use the name of Jesus Christ to cast this devil out." Bridge felt terror for his wife, as she was the center of the expulsion.

"In the name of Christ, we drive you away now, evil spirits, satanic powers!" The priest shouted the last words. He then reached out and touched Catherine with his hand, and she jerked on the chair as he touched her. His touch lit a fire under Catherine, and her body jerked so violently, she broke free from the ropes. Without warning, she charged at one of the assistants, scratching his face and tearing at his eyes. The remaining assistants rushed to his rescue and tried to pin her down, but Catherine was too fast and too strong.

"The sacred Sign of the Cross commands you." Tobey's voice echoed around the room. He managed to touch Catherine's forehead with a cross, and she collapsed to the floor, arms spread wide. She appeared lifeless.

Bridge cried out and fell to the floor by her side. What had the priest done to his wife? He shook her, but she was unresponsive. Did this priest really possess the powers he claimed to have? Or was he a fraud? At this point, all rational thought and reason had been driven from Bridge's mind.

"I can feel her pulse," one of the assistants exclaimed, kneeling beside them.

Bridge felt hot anger burning in his chest. He swallowed and tried not to escalate the situation. "I called you here for one thing," he squared up to the priest and his men, "and you've turned it into a bloodbath."

"How dare you—." Tobey began, but Bridge cut him off.

"Get out!" His voice was coarse, eyes bloodshot. "Get out! All of you!"

The priest nodded and bowed his head, and took a step towards the door. Before departing, he smiled and said, "When the unclean spirit has gone out of a man, he passes through waterless places seeking rest, but he finds none. Then he says, I will return to my house from which I came. And when he comes and finds it empty, swept and put in order, then he goes and brings with him seven other spirits eviler than himself. They enter and dwell there, and the last state of that man becomes worse than the first. You have been warned, Bridge." He held on to his crucifix as he walked away; his assistants followed suit. Bridge held his wife on the floor as he watched them leave.

21

Christine hadn't slept a wink all night. The phone call from Kenneth had jarred her, and she couldn't wrap her head around how Rachel had made it all the way to Mecklenburg County. She put on a pot of coffee and sat at the table, trying to clear her head and make sense of what was happening. Just as she poured her cup, the doorbell rang. It was barely 6 am. Who could be calling?

She opened the door to find Ben's therapist, Marshall, standing in her doorway holding two takeout cups of coffee. Christine looked at him in surprise.

"I figured you might need one of these," he began, handing one to her. "May I come in?"

Christine opened the door numbly and allowed him inside. Then, as they sat at the kitchen table, he spoke.

"I don't know if it's a good idea to say this to you, but I'm just going to say it anyway. I followed the news story on the death of Ben's parents, and personally, I feel there's something fishy about it. But, of course, you can say that is my opinion…." He paused and took a deep breath. "I feel I'm talking too much. All I want to say is I want to help find Rachel." His stare lingered.

"That's what you came here to talk to me about?" Christine looked surprised, and Marshall looked sheepish. "Well, alright. I could use some help. Especially from a professional like yourself." She sighed. "I know where Rachel is. I got a bizarre phone call last night from Virginia."

Marshall looked relieved and curious. "Who called you?"

"Rachel and Ben's old neighbors. The house where the tragedy took place. Rachel is there with them now. They found her last night."

"Well, are you going out there?" Marshall inquired.

"Right away. You coming with me? It's a long drive. Let's go."

"Rachel? Are you alright? You've been asleep." Flicking the lights on and opening the blinds, Kenneth sat on the edge of the bed as Rachel lay there, blinking and shielding her eyes with her hands.

"Well, it's after twelve. Your aunt rang. She's already on the road and will be here by this evening. Maybe once we're all together, we can figure out what's going on." Rachel turned on her side and peered around the room, yawning. She felt exhausted.

"My dad and I have been talking. We think it's a good idea to tell your aunt what's been going on." Rachel nodded weakly, her face pale.

"We'll be in the kitchen, okay? You take your time and meet us out there when you feel ready." Kenneth closed the door quietly behind him.

Kenneth and his father had spent the morning drenched in their own anxiety. How would they explain Rachel's strange appearance if the police questioned them? How were they going to explain things to Christine?

Kenneth joined his father at the dining table as they waited. For what felt like the millionth time, they revisited the facts. Mr. Patterson remembered the newspaper clippings he had shown Rachel all of those months ago. He went to retrieve the papers and came back with the book Rachel had discovered in the basement of the old manor. He flipped through the pages and remembered that they couldn't read the words. His hand stopped suddenly, mid-page.

"Kenneth!" He called out immediately, excited.

"I'm right here, dad. You have to keep it down. We don't want to alarm Rachel." Kenneth hushed him, then went to his side to see what he had discovered.

"You need to see this." Mr. Patterson pointed to the page.

"What is this? It's all gibberish." Kenneth sighed, irritated.

"These are the initials of the Midori family," Mr. Patterson said without looking up at his son.

"Sorry?" Kenneth frowned, his mind trying to gather all the snippets of information his dad constantly blabbered on about, attempting to keep track of his endless threads of unknown details and piece them together.

Only then did he realize his dad was holding the book Rachel had brought to them a year ago. "Wait, the Midoris that grandpa used to tell me about? Dark magic?"

Mr. Patterson nodded.

"And this clue has been here all of this time!" Kenneth exclaimed.

"Nobody has seen it until now." The old man raised his gray eyebrows.

"We need to find out more about these Midoris." Kenneth shook his head in amazement. Their curiosity was piqued now.

The afternoon passed quickly as they worked on deciphering the book and making sense of what was going on. Then, the sound of a car pulling up to the front of the house caught their attention. They both rushed to the window and watched as Rachel's aunt, brother, and a strange man exited the vehicle. Mr. Patterson walked to the front door to meet them.

"Hi, Christine. I'm Jake Patterson. We've been chatting on the phone." He stuck out his hand, and Christine forced a smile and reciprocated his gesture. Ben rushed and hugged the old man. "How are you doing, buddy?"

"Fine." Ben smiled.

"And you are?" He reached out again to shake the stranger's hand.

"Hi, uhh, I'm a therapist. A friend of the family." An awkward pause filled the air.

"Do you have a name?" Mr. Patterson asked.

"Yes! Marshall, Marshall Hanning," the therapist laughed.

"Well, nice to meet you. I'm Jake. This is my son, Kenneth."

Kenneth had been peering out of the door curiously. "Well, why don't you all come on in! Rachel's inside."

The evening light streaming through the window felt warm on her skin as she shifted to the other side of the bed. She lay there half-awake, barely aware that the bedroom door had opened and she had visitors. Mr. Patterson had walked Christine and Ben to her room while Marshall waited in the sitting room. Christine let out an audible gasp at the state of her niece.

"Oh my goodness. What happened to her?"

"I don't think we want to discuss that here. And Rachel should probably rest. So let's go to the sitting room, shall we?" Patterson offered.

As they all situated themselves in the sitting room, silence penetrated the air. Christine felt like she was still in shock. A hysterical laugh broke the silence, and to her horror, Christine realized it was coming from her, as she was overcome by the strangeness of the situation. Sitting in this room, with these near strangers, figuring out what had happened with her niece.

Mr. Patterson looked back and forth between Christine and Ben, wondering where to start. He disliked being in uncomfortable situations like this. He worried about sounding crazy. What if she didn't believe him and decided to call the police? He had practiced the story in his head, waiting for Christine's arrival, but saying it out loud now seemed ludicrous.

"Well, if no one is going to explain what's going on, I'll break the ice." Christine shifted in her seat on the sofa. "What on earth happened to Rachel? And how did she magically reappear in Virginia?"

"Yes, that's what we want to discuss. Well, I'll let my father start." Kenneth looked uncomfortably at his father.

Mr. Patterson sighed. "I believe that everyone in this room is concerned about Rachel. Clearly, she is not well. What I am about to tell you might sound insane."

"If I hear this one more time—." Christine burst out.

They all turned and looked at her, and she shut her mouth in a tight line, allowing Mr. Patterson to continue.

"The Lady of the Lake—." He began, but Christine interrupted him again.

"The Lady of what? Are you the one feeding the kids with this cock-and-bull story?" Christine yelled and made to stand up, but Marshall guided her back into her seat and hushed her to stay calm.

"It is not a cock-and-bull story. We watched Kate, your brother's wife, go mad because of the Lady of the Lake. Everyone in this county knows this house was haunted. Until you guys showed up, no one went near the lake, and no one went near the house. The Lady of the Lake is powerful, and she can take over your mind and make you see terrible things. She's nearly impossible to fight. We believe Rachel is fighting her now." Mr. Patterson frowned.

"Wait a minute. Are you saying Rachel might go mad just like her mother?" Marshall cut in.

"Are we supposed to believe this? I thought you would be reasonable!" Christine asked furiously; she seemed bent on not encouraging the fantasy the old man was spewing.

"Christine, I think we should listen to what he has to say." Marshall gave her a stern look.

Mr. Patterson surveyed the room, then stood up and walked to the kitchen, returning with the book and the box of old newspaper clippings. "I understand it sounds crazy. And if I was in your shoes, I don't know if I would believe it either. But you have to because Rachel needs us, and her life depends on it." He dropped the box onto Christine's lap. "See this one? This is an article dated back to 1923, covering the haunting of this house. But, unfortunately, Kate and John weren't the only people to experience this tragedy. The family that moved here in the early 1900s suffered the same fate."

Christine began flipping through the pages, the words blurring before her eyes. A deep feeling of dread filled her stomach, and she was silent as Mr. Patterson's words began to sink in. Then, one of the words from a headline jumped out at her. *Twins.* She glanced over at Ben, and it all clicked.

"Wait, so are these kids that Ben sees?"

"Those would be Michael Bridge's children. Unfortunately, they were killed by their mother in the same fashion as your brother."

"Stabbed?" Christine's jaw dropped.

"Yes."

"Okay. Enough of the gloom and doom. What is the way forward?" Marshall asked.

Mr. Patterson dropped the large old book with the Midori initials on it into the box. "This is our only lead.

We've uncovered something in this book earlier, and things are beginning to make sense."

"What is this? Major Michael Bridge's Journal?" Christine read the cover out loud. Her head felt fuzzy, swimming with new information. Nothing was making sense.

"We don't think it's a journal. We believe it is a book of spells that the Midoris used to perform dark magic," he informed them. "When Kenneth was younger, he used to be fascinated by stories of the Midoris; he'd sit on my dad's lap every Saturday just to hear a tale of dark magic. The Midoris were a gypsy family that settled here in Mecklenburg County in the early 1800s; for whatever reason, they must have become involved with the Bridge family and thus the book."

"So, we possibly have a spellbook?" Marshall asked, feeling like he was still in the dark. "I'm trying to understand how this is connected to Rachel."

"Conjuring demons, or better stated, the spirits of the dead. It's coming to me now." Mr. Patterson paused and closed his eyes. "So one might see the Lady of the Lake, but in the true sense, these are combinations of different demonic forces haunting the Manor." The old man was intrigued that he could decipher that information quickly. He paced around the room as Marshall and Christine flipped through the book and tried to decode its contents. Ben sat quietly on the sofa, swinging his legs back and forth beneath him.

"So, how do we move forward? How does this information help us?" Christine asked softly, motivated into action.

"I think we're getting somewhere, but I am also not sure where to go from here." Mr. Patterson's expression looked bleak. They needed to help Rachel, but they couldn't exactly go to the police or take her to a hospital. They were going to have to figure this out on their own.

"Poor Rachel," Christine murmured, remembering Rachel's nightmares and how she wandered the house at night. "I can't imagine going through all of this trauma and now living in this nightmare."

"Rachel!" Ben yelled out excitedly. They all turned their attention to the hallway as Rachel emerged, face pale. She looked at them with a strange expression and slowly entered the room. Christine felt her heart burst with gratitude that she was safe and rushed forward to meet her. As she approached, she realized that Rachel's hair was wet, a trail of water following her into the room.

"Oh honey, your hair is wet," Christine said softly, grabbing her and hugging her tightly. She was too excited to hold her niece in her arms to notice as Rachel's right hand emerged from behind her back, holding a knife. She didn't take notice until the blade plunged into her shoulder and her niece's teeth clenched firmly on her neck.

22

MECKLENBURG COUNTY, 1869

Everyone came out for one of the biggest horse races in Mecklenburg County. A stirring of excitement rippling through the stands. The sport was growing in popularity, and the townspeople reveled in the opportunity to place bets and win money. Bridge frequently partook in these bets and came to the arena often to join the festivities.

He had a favorite horse called Leigh, and he admired her speed and strong beauty. But sport wasn't the only thing that drew Bridge to the arena. The space was commonly known as the meeting point for shady business, and Bridge often met with the Sheriff and the Mayor in a private invitation-only room. The room had no name, just a number: 30.

Bridge entered number 30 and spotted his acquaintances already seated at a table in the corner, smoking, and gambling. He removed his jacket and approached.

"Bridge, what an honor to see you in our midst again." The Sheriff laughed and rose to shake his hand.

"Bridge, you want to join in?" The Mayor offered to deal him cards.

"Not today, thank you." Bridge declined and removed his hat. At the moment, he wanted an escape from the troubles at home, and he didn't feel like playing.

"How are things going at home? I've heard about some trouble with your wife." The Sheriff broke the ice.

"Yes, you heard right, Sheriff McCaughey. Unfortunately, things are not going well at home. I have serious troubles with my wife. The sorts of troubles I have never seen any man have before." He sighed and signaled to the barman for some scotch.

"Is it that serious?" The Sheriff turned to him and raised an eyebrow.

"Yes, it is. A demon has plagued my wife, and I don't know what to do." He gulped his scotch and slammed the glass on the table.

The men around the table didn't know how to react to this bold statement. One started laughing, and another looked at Bridge with pity in his eyes. The Mayor looked incredulous. "Demon, you say?"

"Yes, an evil spirit has overtaken her. I don't know how else to explain it." He looked around the table as if challenging them to prove him wrong. "You all might laugh, but I feel like my home is cursed."

In the silence that followed, Bridge took the opportunity to take another swig of his scotch.

"No, that can't be." The Sheriff patted him on the back. "What is going on exactly? There has to be a reasonable explanation for this."

"Well, this isn't easy to talk about. Mostly I've noticed that she is short-tempered, and her eyes sometimes glow green. She's stronger than she used to be and more aggressive. I've witnessed her bullying the children. They're only eight, you know. I consulted a psychiatrist, but he said he didn't believe these were signs of mental illness. So I've hired a nurse because I'm worried about leaving the children alone with her."

The men stared at Bridge with wide eyes, gathering closer as he spoke. No one was laughing now.

Bridge slipped the bottle of scotch under his jacket as he left the room just before the race was due to begin. He made his way to the fence and watched as Leigh was announced, and the audience cheered. He closed his eyes and prayed for a big win, then made his way into the stands to his seat.

"You bet on Leigh again? I think her odds are low today. My bet is on the white horse over there. What's his name again?" The Mayor took a seat beside Bridge.

"Pierce," Bridge said, pointing down at the racebook in his hand. "Look, if you're sitting here because you want to keep talking about my wife, it's no use. I don't have anything more to say about the situation other than that I am strong. I survived the war, I can certainly survive this." He sounded defiant as he took a long swig of scotch, this time straight from the bottle.

"Actually, I'm here because I noticed you grabbed that bottle of scotch." They both shared a laugh. Bridge felt surprised to hear laughter coming from him in a time like this. "Have you heard about the new studs imported from Boston? In no time, they are going to be the best in the county."

"Yes, I've heard, but it's just a rumor. Most times, I don't take news like that seriously," Bridge said. "They're all average horse breeders. I still bet my money on Leigh, anytime, any day." He returned his gaze to the race track.

"She certainly is a beauty," the Mayor sighed. "I pray you to find peace, my friend. I hope your wife heals quickly from this ailment." He squeezed Bridge gently on the shoulder and walked off. Bridge looked out at the track, pondering over the next step to take.

On the ride home, Bridge sat in the carriage with his head in his hands. He was quite inebriated, and bumping down the road was not helping his situation. As the night deepened, he watched the stars twinkle in the night sky. Warmth wrapped around Bridge as he appreciated God's gifts to mankind. Although, this feeling could have also come from the scotch.

"We're here," he ordered the driver to stop.

"That would be 10 cents, sir." The driver tipped his hat as Bridge stumbled out of the carriage. Bridge placed the 10 cent piece in his hand, and the carriage driver sped off, leaving Bridge to stagger all alone to his house.

As he approached the darkened manor and weaved towards the front porch, he didn't notice the eerie silence. In his mind, he saw his children playing out front and smiled. As he approached, the wind began to howl, and the house creaked and shuddered. It was so dark, the moon was the only source of light shining down.

He struggled to get to the porch as he staggered on the grass leading to the manor's entrance. "Catherine!" he yelled out.

"Emily," he yelled out again. "Yvonne! Come on, children. Daddy needs your help." He chuckled and fell face-first onto the grass. The wind was picking up now, making it more difficult for him to regain his footing. He knew he shouldn't be drinking so much, but it was the only thing that was helping him cope right now. With alcohol, Bridge was always at the crossroad between being adventurous and being plain stupid, like he was now.

He struggled to crawl toward the door. "A whole bottle of scotch." He laughed to himself. "I drank a whole bottle of scotch. Catherine, you should come to see this," he whispered.

And she appeared, walking slowly towards him from the direction of the lake, dressed in white. Bridge's vision was blurry, but he knew it was his wife.

"Catherine," he said softly, relieved. "Come on, Catherine. Take me up."

Catherine approached, arms outstretched. She stared down at him, face unmoving, eyes cold.

"Where are the children?" he asked.

"I'll take you to them." She helped him up and put his arm around her shoulder, guiding him down to the lake.

156

Once at the shore, she released him, and he fell to the ground.

"What are we doing down here? Where is the nurse?" Hitting the ground seemed to wake him up, and he peered up at her with confusion.

"Wait. How did you..?" He tried to stand up, but Catherine used her left foot to pin him on the ground.

He could see clearly now; her white gown was stained with blood, and it brought him back to his senses. He felt his stomach drop, and he knew something terrible must have happened. He tried to break free, but he was too weak to move. She grabbed him by the hair and turned his face to gaze at the lake.

Bridge squeezed his eyes shut, afraid of what he might see. When he tried to open them, tears blurred his vision, but he could still make out the horrific scene before him. Two small bodies floated on the surface of the lake, bobbing against each other as the water rippled around them. He let out a painful wail and closed his eyes again, hoping he was trapped in a drunken nightmare and this was all a dream.

Catherine grabbed his hair again and turned his head to face her, and now he could see the knife glinting in her hand. "You're next," she told him.

Her eyes flashed green, and he was suddenly overcome with rage. He was going to kill her, and this new vengeance helped him struggle to his feet. But he was no match for her strength, and she knocked him back to the ground, delighting in his weakness.

Thunder roared through the sky, and as the lightning flashed, Catherine wielded the knife over her head and brought it down with a terrible blow. The blade pierced

Bridge directly in the heart. He flinched and twitched as she stared into his eyes, watching the blue fade away. Dying was a messy process, and pain was inevitable.

There was wild hunger in Catherine's eyes as Bridge grew still. She dragged his lifeless body slowly into the lake and smiled as the water turned red with his blood.

23

Christine stumbled back in shock, pain shooting through her shoulder. Only now did she see the green light emanating from her niece's cold eyes. Everyone rushed toward Christine, except Ben, who remained seated on the sofa. Rachel kept her aunt captive, surveying everyone, the bloody knife gripped in her fist.

"Come any closer, and I'll stab her again," Rachel threatened with a growl. She wore a devilish smile on her face, urging them to back away. They slowly retreated into the sitting room.

"Trust me, you don't want to do this," Mr. Patterson pleaded as he inched slowly backward. Everyone appeared to be in shock and fearful of what Rachel would do next. The only one who didn't show any signs of fear was Ben. Ben had slipped off of the couch and was making his way forward to meet Rachel.

"No!" Christine called out in desperation, reaching for him.

"It's me you want, Lady of the Lake. Leave my sister alone." He was fast, already in front of Rachel. Marshall also tried to call out to him, but he ignored the therapist.

For the first time in Christine's life, she was close to death. Her body felt numb, and her head was swimming. As her mind wandered, she thought of all of the ways she could have died. This certainly wasn't how she had thought she was going to go. Who would have thought Virginia was nothing but trouble for the McAllister family? Who would have thought Rachel would become possessed? Not Christine. All she had wanted to do was protect the kids from harm.

"Stop this now!" Kenneth yelled and charged at her with his fists flailing, but Rachel was ready. She dodged the blows, and Christine seized the opportunity and shoved Rachel with her other shoulder. She felt a sudden, dizzying sense of liberation.

"Don't try to fight her!" She shouted. "Don't harm her!" She didn't want Rachel to be injured in any way. In her mind, there had to be a way for them to salvage the situation. She turned to Mr. Patterson, who was preoccupied looking out for his son.

Kenneth fell to the floor as Rachel dodged his attempt, and she turned on him just as Christine broke free. Marshall hurriedly grabbed Ben and dove out of the way. Kenneth scrambled backward, fighting hard to regain his breath. He straightened up, mixed emotions crossing his face, and he shook his head vigorously.

"You can stop this madness, Rachel. I know you're still in there. Remember, you are strong, and you have the power to overcome this!"

Rachel held the knife tighter and arched her body backward, a flash of a smile on her face.

Dark clouds enveloped the sky above them, blocking out the fading light. Rachel took her chance and charged at

Kenneth, but he evaded her attack and landed one fist straight to her face. She fell to the floor, and the knife fell out of her grasp. They all watched in horror as Rachel laughed, popped her neck, and landed back on her feet. It was as if Kenneth hadn't even hit her.

Rachel lunged for the knife and felt her hand connecting with the cold metal as she went for Kenneth one more time in a smooth motion. Mr. Patterson screamed and tried to enter the fray, but Christine held him back. She was torn between protecting Kenneth and ensuring that Rachel didn't get hurt.

Kenneth couldn't evade her this time, and the knife made contact with one of his thighs, creating a thin horizontal line of blood. Rachel drew back and circled for a second attempt, but Mr. Patterson broke free and threw his body between Kenneth and Rachel. She struck, wounding him on the hip, and he fell to the floor in pain, taking out Rachel on the way down. Christine screamed, and Marshall rushed to help the older man.

As Rachel remained on the floor unconscious, they checked to see if Mr. Patterson was okay.

"Do you feel hurt?"

"I've been better." He managed to get the words out with a grimace.

The clouds didn't pass, and the sky grew darker as night fell. Just then, the lights in the house began to flicker. They looked at each other nervously, unsure of what would happen next.

"The Lady of the Lake is angry," Ben said in a low tone. They turned to him, surprised at his revelation.

"It's not safe here," Mr. Patterson gasped. He struggled to stand up.

"Take it easy," Christine said sharply. She hurriedly grabbed a chair from the kitchen for Mr. Patterson to sit on.

"He is right. You need to get out of here. It's not safe." Kenneth concurred.

"And what? Leave my niece here?" Christine exclaimed angrily. A steady stream of blood was trickling down her shoulder, and she looked like she might pass out. Marshall rushed to assist her.

"You're bleeding a lot. We need to stop this flow. Do you have a first aid kit?"

Just then, the lights flickered one last time and went out, leaving the house in near-total darkness. Kenneth grabbed his cell phone out of his back pocket and clicked on the flashlight. The light was weak but enough to illuminate the scene.

Mr. Patterson groaned. "Kenneth, go grab the first aid kit. It's under the kitchen sink."

The atmosphere grew colder, and tension filled the air. Both Christine and Mr. Patterson needed medical attention, and quickly. Christine bit her lower lip in an attempt to prevent her from crying out in pain. But she still screamed as Marshall used antiseptic and dressed the wound.

Once Christine and Mr. Patterson were attended to as best they could, they turned their attention back to the matter at hand.

"I know she's not a current threat, but we need to put our heads together and figure out how to free Rachel," Christine said with authority.

"I still believe there is a connection with the book. We just need to keep deciphering it and determine how to move forward." Mr. Patterson suggested as Kenneth searched for some candles.

As they brainstormed how to proceed, Ben's small voice penetrated the darkness.

"We don't need to decode the book. We just need to destroy it."

They all stared at him in surprise, sitting there on the sofa illuminated by soft candlelight. Christine started heading towards the couch when the candles flickered and went out.

"Aunt Christine?" Ben called out in fear. Panic filled the room, and Christine couldn't feel for Ben on the sofa in the commotion.

"Ben!" She cried.

Kenneth switched on his cell phone flashlight and shined it in the direction of the couch. Empty. Then he pointed the beam to where Rachel was on the floor. Except she was no longer there.

"She's gone!" Kenneth yelled. "Rachel, stop!"

They took off through the house searching for Rachel and Ben. Mr. Patterson rummaged around on the table for the book as the rest of the group ran outside.

"It was just here! Where is it?" He shoved the contents of the coffee table onto the floor and tossed throw pillows off of the sofa. He caught sight of the moon rising through the window and felt a chill run through his body. The scene reminded him of the night that Kate killed John.

"Dad! Dad, she has the book!" Kenneth turned back to yell, and Mr. Patterson ran outside to join the pursuit.

Rachel carried Ben on her back and moved with increasing speed towards the lake. Christine ran with tears in her eyes, chasing after her niece and nephew. She had already thought she had lost Rachel, and now she might lose Ben as well.

Kenneth appeared to be the only one closing in, as the rest were lagging behind. The lake was shimmering ahead of them, and they all knew that nothing good would happen once they reached the lake. Kenneth saw his chance to make contact and jumped forward, but he missed her legs and landed hard on the ground. This gave her an advantage as he picked himself up and continued running.

Rachel reached the lake before the others, dropped Ben on the ground, and dragged him behind her as she waded into the water. Ben struggled to breathe as his head continuously dipped beneath the surface. In one hand, Rachel held firmly to the book. In the other, she held onto Ben. She felt him struggling behind her but kept proceeding deeper into the lake.

Kenneth reached the water and dove in, swimming furiously to the pair of bodies ahead of him. "Stop!" Kenneth shouted, seeing Ben gasping for breath. He made a final attempt to reach them and surprised himself by making contact with Ben's small ankle. A struggle followed, but Kenneth managed to wrestle the book free from Rachel's hand. He tossed it to his father, who had swum out into the water, and worked next on freeing Ben. It seemed like it was no use. Rachel's grip was tight.

Mr. Patterson reached the shore and held the book up victoriously. To his surprise, he realized it wasn't even wet.

"How are we going to destroy it?" Christine asked. "And quickly! Rachel is not far behind."

They all turned their attention back to the water, seeing that Rachel was only a few yards from the shore, Kenneth trying to keep up behind her.

"I brought a lighter." Mr. Patterson placed the book on top of a rock and held the flame to the pages. Nothing happened.

Rachel reached the shore with a furious cry and came charging towards the group, green eyes flashing. Then, out of nowhere, Marshall slammed into her from the side, taking her down and pinning her to the ground.

At long last, the pages caught fire, and the book went up in flames. Marshall could feel her losing strength beneath him, the green slowing fading from her eyes. They all collectively held their breath as the book burned.

Kenneth carried Ben from the lake, and they rejoined the group. Ben was weak, but he was going to make a full recovery.

As the book turned to ashes, Christine knelt next to Rachel and felt her pulse. Her skin felt cold and clammy, and her pulse was faint. But she was alive. Christine ran a hand soothingly over her head.

"You'll be alright, baby."

Rachel's eyelids fluttered but didn't open. Her skin was pale, almost translucent. Christine held her in her arms, rocking back and forth, glad that it was finally over.

24

FIVE MONTHS LATER

Christine and Marshall Hanning were engaged to be married and bought a house together in Chicago. Rachel still didn't know how she felt about the arrangement, but Ben seemed to take a liking to his old therapist. To Rachel's delight, Kenneth had agreed to spend his summer in Chicago to help Rachel recover fully.

Rachel and Ben were settling into life in Chicago, having completed the school year and both feeling like somewhat normal kids. Ben had stopped talking to the twins, and he was making more of an effort to engage at school and speak up at home. It appeared that extra love and care were what he needed to open up.

Rachel felt indebted to Christine for standing up and fighting for them, and Christine was still grateful to have them in her life, especially after everything they had been through. In fact, she believed having the kids in her care was the best thing that had ever happened to her.

They still had a lot to work through as a family, and it was not easy to forget all of the bad memories and move on, but it would come with time. Rachel felt lucky that they had Christine and Marshall to guide them. She was no longer having terrible nightmares and had felt peace knowing that both the Lady of the Lake and her mother were finally free.

As they stepped into their new house in the suburbs of Chicago, Luna, their new puppy, took off up the stairs, Ben trailing behind her. The house wasn't quite old but could use a good cleaning before moving in their belongings.

"It's time to get this house cleaned and organized! What a great opportunity to bond as a family," Christine said. And they got to work.

"How happy are you about this place?" Marshall asked her, massaging her shoulders.

"It's good. Actually, it's great. It reminds me of the house John and I grew up in."

"Oh yeah?" Marshall raised his eyebrows, smiling at her.

"Yeah." She kissed him.

Rachel and Ben carried boxes from the moving container outside into the house. Christine took a break, watching the kids as they ran back and forth, leaning on the porch railing and sipping a coffee. She laughed as Ben rushed to get the smallest boxes. She noticed one box sitting on the porch that had belonged to her brother, John. She set down her coffee and decided to rummage through it. She saw a letter in the box addressed to Rachel, and she set it aside. The next time Rachel was on the porch, she slipped it to her.

Rachel took a deep breath as Christine entered the house to give her some alone time. It was a handwritten letter from her father. Rachel's heart felt heavy. Whatever was in the letter seemed like his last words to her. Slowly she opened it and began to read:

My dear Rachel,

I'm writing this letter and praying that you will wake up and get to read it one day. I pray every day that you will wake up and heal our broken hearts.

I am sorry that I wasn't there for you all the time. When you wake up, I promise that we will always be by your side, and nothing will ever drift us apart. There is so much that I want to share with you. You make me so proud, you bring me so much joy, and you're the best daughter I could have ever asked for.

I love you,

Dad

Rachel felt her heart lurch with love. She took a deep breath and held it for a moment before saying the words she wished she had told him before he died.

"I love you too, daddy."

The End.

Thank you for reading *The Haunting of Bridge Manor – The Trilogy.* It means a lot to me that you bought my book and I hope you enjoyed reading it!

If you liked this book, I would really appreciate an honest review on Amazon. I love to read what you have to say.

Scan the QR Code with your smartphone and leave me your feedback!

GET EXLUSIVE FREE NOVELLA

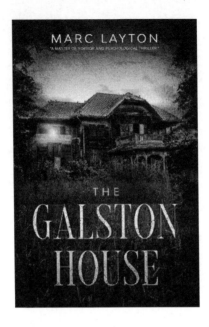

Don't forget to subscribe to my newsletter and join my VIP Readers Club for information on upcoming releases, plus you receive a free copy of The Galston House!

Are you ready? Take out your camera app, make sure it can clearly see the code, and wait for the notification to appear. That's it!

ALSO BY MARC LAYTON

THE HIDDEN GRAVEYARD
A SUSPENSEFUL SHORT STORY

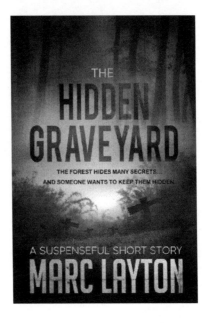

The forest hides many secrets… and someone wants to keep them hidden.

Twenty years after their parent's tragic disappearance, brothers Damian and Liam are on the hunt for the truth. Traveling to the shadowy woodland where that fateful day occurred, nothing could have prepared them for what old forces they were about to stumble into.

Shrouded in mystery, the forest hides many dangers and has swallowed many souls. Determined to investigate the cause of their parents' disappearance, Damian and Liam must sift through the stories and decide who they can trust… and who might be hiding something.

And after the pair attract the attention of an elusive enemy who haunts the dark and ominous woods, the brothers will need to use all of their wits if they want to uncover the truth and make it out alive...

Can Damian and Liam find out what happened to their parents all those years ago? Or will they become the forest's next victims?

Perfect for fans of spine-chilling paranormal mysteries with suspense that will have you hanging from every page, The Hidden Graveyard **is a riveting short read that will delight fans of classic and creepy ghost stories. Scroll up and grab your copy now!**

READ NOW! Take out your camera app, make sure it can clearly see the code, and wait for the notification to appear. That's it!

THE TASTER
INVESTIGATING HORROR SERIES

A labyrinthian cellar. A priceless wine collection. And a vengeful spirit who guards it for eternity.

Hidden in the darkest depths of the famous wine taster Matthew Boudin's cellar lies a secret – a collection of some of the rarest and most expensive wines the world has ever seen. Guarded by a maze of pitch-black corridors – and the embalmed corpse of the late Boudin himself – the collection has stood untouched for years.

Professor Aldous Crane doesn't believe in ghosts. Despite writing about the occult for over thirty years, he views their stories as a bit of fun and nothing more. But when he's called to investigate Boudin's infamous cellar, he soon realizes that the truth is something far more sinister.

If you love thrilling supernatural and occult stories packed with hair-raising suspense and tension which will keep you on the edge of your seat, then you won't want to miss *The Taster*. Grab your copy today!

READ NOW! Take out your camera app, make sure it can clearly see the code, and wait for the notification to appear. That's it!

SLEEPLESS
THE EVERGREEN MOTEL SERIES

Best Horror Book of the Month April 2020 Award - manybooks.net

Kyle's threatening message hang in the air as Aly hits the country road, desperate to find safety. Her violent ex-boyfriend persists to hunt her down. The farther she escapes from Kyle, the more threatening his messages become.

He will stop at nothing to get her back.

Aly constantly reaches for the gun in her pocket — the only thing that is keeping her sane. After two hours of non-stop driving, the tension of the day starts to weigh heavy on her. She turns into the parking lot of The Evergreen Motel, a sleepy reprieve nestled in the woods.

However, what she thought was the perfect refuge slowly turns into something more sinister. The moment Aly lays down to sleep, strange things begin to occur. Paranoia, nightmares, and loud screams cut through the air.

READ NOW! Take out your camera app, make sure it can clearly see the code, and wait for the notification to appear. That's it!

ABOUT THE AUTHOR

Marc Layton's passion for writing spine-chilling stories full of intrigue and suspense was born out of his travels around the globe. He felt inspired by the places he visited and the people he connected with and was motivated to pursue writing so he could share these stories with the world. A voracious reader of thriller and horror stories himself, it was only natural that he would dive into this genre.

Join Marc on Facebook for updates, fun conversations, and giveaways.

Take out your camera app, make sure it can clearly see the code, and wait for the notification to appear. That's it!

Printed in Great Britain
by Amazon

45963198R00101